The Fatal Stillness Of The Sun

Benjamin Weberink

This is a work of fiction. Names, characters, places, and incidents either are the product of the author's imagination or are used fictitiously. Any resemblance to actual persons, living or dead, events, or locales is entirely coincidental.

Copyright © 2024 by Benjamin Weberink

All rights reserved. No part of this book may be reproduced or used in any manner without written permission of the copyright owner except for the use of quotations in a book review.

First paperback edition October 2024

Book design by Benjamin Weberink

ISBN 979-12-210-7244-0 (paperback)

Chapter 1
With A Blink

It's draining. The bleak colours of the room find solace in the brown walls. Cigarette butts stain the carpet with heavy black strokes. I know this place. It used to be my safe haven, a delicate abode where I could unravel myself and lay it down with ease. But it no longer is.

The street is quiet tonight. City lights shimmer in the distance within a thick air of regret. The bar downstairs repeats its usual low hum of conversation. I couldn't escape this place even if I wanted to. It is life etched into my skin. I am an insect. Hope struggles to bloom in the cracks of this place. People are desperate. Desperate for practically anything. Shades crawl across the ceiling. I walk over to my bed. Clothes are sprawled out all over the place. They look like body bags. I reach inside my jeans pocket, and I feel around for my lighter, but to no avail. I never wished to be like this. I never wished to be drowning. A shallow empty shell of a man with God knows what to live for. I would take pill after pill. I would take pill after pill, wash them down with bottles of vodka and rum. I would swallow them with the strongest alcohol I have. But the migraine would prevail. Always the fucking headaches. I turn around frantically as if caught by my own thoughts. I walk over to the window. I've never felt this burnt out. I look out, down on the people walking below. I would give anything to peek into their existences, to see what troubles they face, what other shit the world has brought upon us, so I don't feel alone for once. Just for once.

'What would she have said?' I think

Here it is again. I can't get over it. The remembrance influences every breath I take. It's been a while now. Nearly a year since she left. Her voice still spirals away in my head.

You turn me inside out.

I was a grave digger. I was digging up trauma in her excavation to bring her past up in my favour. Reusing until there was nothing she could hold on to. It's good she decided to leave when she could. I know I changed her. Changed her for the worse. And how could I have done that? I would sit there, keeping her quiet about my drinking. And I would waste unspent time, rejecting any possibility of comfort. I look around the room with heavy eyes. I try to find my house keys. I need to get out. I need to free myself from the shackles binding me, loosen the delicate threads that weave me to her. I see my keys. I grab them with force, mistakenly kicking the table footloose. It would always happen. I find it difficult to control myself. I can never hold back my sudden anger. It feels like a disease plaguing my mind. I have to learn how to embrace a mending scar and not pry it open every chance I get. She would keep asking me to let her go. No, not out of fear, but out of sheer pain. I didn't even see her leave. I was passed out. I honestly don't blame her.

The apartment isn't big. Entering brings you directly into the painfully sharp-lit kitchen. A stink pulses from the sink. I never got it fixed. I can live with it. The table leaning against the wall has two chairs, with a simple patterned cushion on one of them. There isn't anything on the table. Turning to the right is the small bedroom, with a bed tucked under the square window, and a closet on the opposite wall. I like to keep the lights off. The darkness resonates within me. I don't have anything up on the walls, just a couple of bookshelves to hold whatever assorted material my mind craves. Turning left from the kitchen is the bathroom. A sort of walk-in shower with a broken faucet. That also has to be fixed. I am not in a state to worry about anything other than her. It's hard to put into words, but that's how I want it to be.

Sometimes I tear at your flesh, like barbed wire.

Her vicious changes didn't come lightly to me either. She started drinking. It wasn't supposed to happen. A bad addiction fueled by another worse addiction. That's what I would say. I remember attempting rehab multiple times throughout this period. It was almost a surprise that I went, considering everything that happened. I thought I wouldn't even have wanted to get better. It felt like I was wasting a possible overdose after she left. And the more I reassure myself, the worse it gets.

The room is no longer clean and symmetrical. It is disorganised and messy. The laundry lies in a heap on the floor. Clothes spill out of the open drawers. I sigh. I sigh because I know I need to do better. But who wants to do anything? The days keep getting longer. There is no end to them. Nights stretch out. The coldness outside is getting worse. I don't know if I can hold on. Money is tight. It's not like I can get a well-paying job around here. Sometimes life offers you absolutely nothing of worth. That's the beauty of it. To find your meaning in the dullness and succumb to it. I look down at my unlaced boots. I feel the blisters on my feet ache as I walk to the exit of the apartment. There's dried blood on the inside sole. I think I'll manage. I always seem to. I hurry to the door, in need of fresh air. It is the middle of February, and the weather is as cold as it was yesterday, and the day before. The wind hasn't settled yet, and it still slams against the window. I grab my jacket and walk towards the stairs. There are no more moments of pure clarity left. Everything comes and goes. I hastily stumble my way down to get out. When will this end.

I step outside. Suddenly cigarette smoke turns into mist, like my breath does in the cold. I shiver and bite my lip, hard.

"Fuck," I whisper.

I touch the inside of my lip. I notice the swelling. To indulge in being alive. I still don't know what to do with myself. It's sacred grief made out of hazy blurs leaking dry at her will. Why did I even come out here? It's the same old concrete building. The same view. The same dusky glow coming from the apartment upstairs, with the same front door and recollection carved into my head. The clouds stand in the way of the stars. It's almost as if they cease to exist. But I see nothing more than a place in need of reparation. Some sort of renewal should suffice nicely. Sadly that would never happen. Neither does it concern me.

It still feels like yesterday. The way she would laugh and stick her middle finger up at the CCTV cameras outside of the complex became a ritual. Our ritual. I would call her the ivory tower. I freed her from her obligations, from her sense of belonging. She liked it that way.

My hands are starting to freeze. Discomfort: from the top point of my fingertips down to my palm. But I like the pain. It reminds me of her long nails slowly going up and down my skin, creating soft red lines like on a tapestry. The intricate details of memory to be reminded of aren't easy. Art that is only displayed once it's been torn up. It lives only in the harmonious rupture in my head. It wasn't easy. She wasn't easy. And nothing will ever be easy. But that's life. That's fucking life. It's a memory to lay waste to.

I walk around the building. I put my attention on anything else. I look to the left of me, then to the right, like I always do. It's the presence that you feel whenever you're alone, and the warmth you feel in your bloodstream that keeps you stable. I turn on my phone. 12:17 a.m. Still early for the usual night. Being sober hasn't helped either. At least I could count on the alcohol to get me to sleep. But I know I'm doing this for my mistakes. For her. I walk even further. I take the usual path around the block, past the stinking black trash containers, and further along the narrow walkway. It leads to the building's car park where I stop and listen to the surroundings speak, to then continue past the rusty metal fence into the communal outdoor area, where I have a full view over the city down below. This is where I come to rest my head sometimes, where noise doesn't find its way inside. It isn't a bad neighbourhood. There are a couple of car robberies and thefts every once in a while, but most of it is reasonably safe. People here stroll around like vampires. They're awake at night and asleep through the sunlight. They blast loud music through the paper-thin walls, and curse and scream deep into the midnight blue. You can smell the bloodlust here, as I stand. There's a hint of violence caught in the atmosphere. Unsettling undertones are created by everything around me with a purpose to subsist. The people around me are good people. I choose to ignore them. I have enough problems as it is. Creating connections only leads to more problems, and more and more shit to bury. The golden lights are bright. The city is still alive tonight. I feel such guilt. Guilt for the ruin I put her in. Guilt for my sins of limiting withdrawal. Of not holding myself accountable. Fucking whatever. What's the point of adding sorrow to it all? I've been out for around twenty minutes now. My hands feel numb to the outside air. I light up a cigarette.

There is a loud noise at the other exit. The soft sound of footsteps catches me by surprise. It's Elias, my upstairs neighbour. Another troubled man. I hear him cry sometimes. Silently and pitifully, as if his tears were burdensome. My eyes meet his.

I nod. I don't get an answer. I get a strong, stiff hug.

He leans around my shoulder, into the back of my head and says "I heard what happened, Noah. I'm so sorry for your loss. I hope the silence isn't too much to deal with"

I don't answer.

"Noah. Are you doing okay?"

All I can do is nod. Painful memories flood in. They overwhelm me with dread and anxiety. Where did it go all wrong?

"Yes," I say, with a slight smile.

There is nothing more but lies. That's what the world owes me. People aren't waiting to care about your troubles. You mean nothing in hindsight. Elias has his shit to deal with. I know he's not waiting for me to be open with him or to let out any pathetic emotion I feel. Besides, I don't mix well with advice. I'm tired of hearing what I should be. I know I can't be someone I'm not. These feelings do more than birth our reveries. They remind us of our mistakes.

"It's just too much to handle all at once. First Mama.

Now this," I say, on the brink of a breakdown, angry at myself for letting myself get vulnerable.

I look at Elias through blurred vision and see his vague outline appear closer.

"I get it," Elias stutters, and is taken aback by the scorching of his voice. "I rarely smile. It isn't worth it sometimes. But sometimes it is."

There are threads of truth in what he's saying. The wind stings my nostrils.

"You'll know you'll be okay. It takes a long fuckin' while"

"I guess it was a sacrifice to atone for being bad."

"No, Noah. It's not that. It's life." He looks at me, and then through me. "Reach out to me when you need it. No one should have to go through this alone, all right?"

But his words don't grasp my attention any more. I'm too busy feeling the breeze caressing my stone-cold face. Holding my breath, my heart starts pounding against my ribs. I stumble backwards. The night's darkness is tiring me. I'll do anything to feel comfort once more.

"Thank you, Elias. Truly. Just for being around... sometimes," I say, jokingly.

He doesn't laugh in response. It was always hard to talk with him; you can't break Elias open.

"Of course. Stay safe," Elias replies.

He shuffles his feet on the concrete. He gives me another long glance and turns around to walk back through the door he came out of.

This leaves me alone. Completely alone with nothing but the surrounding buzz of the streetlights and the quiet rustle of the trees. It never was interchangeable. She was an essential part of me. I've been obliterated.

"Bastard," I curse to myself.

I can feel it rising again. The sudden necessity. At full tilt, I grab the silver lighter out of my pocket and I flick the flame on. Without any second thought, I press it on my forearm. I sear the skin underneath.

"Fucking shit," I say under my breath, dropping the lighter on the pavement.

I wonder why I haven't tried to stop myself before.

I feel at home. I feel the door slam into my face again. I feel the hypocrite within me talk about her drinking patterns. The existential dilemma of being responsible weighs strong on me, but there's nothing I can do. I'm helpless. I see what could have been. But I will never come to my senses again. I touch my arm. I can feel the hotness radiate from it. It hurts, but I feel. I bend over to pick up the lighter, simultaneously grabbing my keys out of my jeans pocket to get back inside. As I look up I see Elias's light turn on. It gleams from his open window on the fourth floor. I head back on the pathway I came from. Past the outdoor area. Past the empty parking spaces and the trash containers. And back to the front steps. I head inside with difficulty. With every step my body aches. My tired footsteps rumble through the building as I make my way upstairs, towards the third floor, juggling the keys around in my hands. I struggle to find the correct one. My eyes have suddenly become heavy. Fatigue takes over. Where is that damn key? And there it is. Its edges are pointy enough to slice through bone. I forcefully push it into the lock. I push the door open. And with this exact push, I black out.

She looked at me with all of her pure intentions. Life and poison. What would I do without you. You've become my bleeding sun.

———

I wake up to the gentle yellow-orange light hitting my face, and the burning sensation that comes with it. It's now 7:36 a.m. Nothing has changed one bit. Sadness slowly starts creeping in as I find myself lying on the floor. The bed is mere centimetres away.

"What happened to me?" I mumble to myself.

I can't remember anything. My memory has been wiped.

I'm not a liar. I promise I don't remember. I'm sick.

It must have been yesterday's somnolent outing. Leah's funeral. I feared I would be unsightly. I remember starting to shuffle between methods of escaping it. But I didn't have anything else. It was unbearable to my naked eye. I showed up in my best attire. I wore the black suit she said I looked good in. There weren't that many people. A couple of faces I knew. A few I didn't. It doesn't matter. They're all the same. People dressed up to mourn. All putting on their best face for someone who needed them when she was still around.

———

The day was dark. Darker than all of February's previous days. Chairs were situated on the grass field. In a half circle. They were pointed towards the casket, which was placed in front of the oak tree. Its elongated branches reached out towards it. It gave the appearance of wanting to hug Leah as she lay there. I know I did. But I couldn't. She was long gone. The tree had shed many of its green leaves. It seemed like it was withering away with the season.

I was the first one present there. I lit up a cigarette, briskly took a hit. I wasn't a heavy smoker. The mere thought of today made me want to be. It reminded me of sex. It reminded me of the way our bodies would fuse.

Spiritually through physical form. How we would make love like ice skaters, leaving behind sharp marks at spots they've been. And how her touch would bring me to my knees. And how we both felt it. We saw the apocalypse in each other's eyes. And hers reflected the candlelight into mine. How her tongue spoke of my name. How could I say bye? How was I expected to overcome my solicitude for her? I couldn't think of an answer.

I walked around the coffin. I let my hand rest on it. The wood fibres were carefully wrapped around the box. I couldn't fathom that Leah was inside. I've never felt a more vast urge to face my confrontations. The coffin did something within me. It filled me with uneasiness. Without notice, the sky abruptly opened. The rain was lashing down, hitting the coffin with loud thumps. I felt like I could hold existence in the palm of my hands, becoming one with the raindrops leaking through the cracks to touch Leah beneath the lid. The tree groaned. It cracked at the pressure of the wind. There were a couple of people now, gathering around to honour Leah. Their umbrellas raised high. Nobody said a word to me. I knew her family did not approve of me. It made my blood boil. I was never treated nicely by them, not even before all the shit came out. I could feel them observing me, scrutinising me. I stayed a distance away from where everyone was situated. I didn't want to intrude. I didn't want to make it seem like I was there to cause any issues. Not today. I didn't feel an ounce of affection for anyone there. I never did. They treated her worse than I did. I won't forget that. Not today. I spotted her family out of the corner of my eye. I loathed the sight of them, laughing around, making it out to be anything but a day for mourning. Her mother's green eyes squinted at the sight of me. She made her way towards me. She wanted a confrontation. It was what she lived off, creating problems where she knew could end up being crowned. But I wasn't going to say shit. She would have had to pull it out of me. She knew she couldn't do that.

"Noah, right? Sorry. I forget names," she said.

"Yes, that's my name," I responded, conveying all possible odium towards her. She looked at me with a surprised face.

"So you're here for Leah too? That's funny."

"Why would that be funny?" I said.

"She didn't talk too nicely about you, Noah."

"Oh. I think—" I started.

But she sharply cut me off.

"Listen, Noah. I don't like you, I think you know that."

"I don't like you either."

"I don't know your relationship with my daughter, and I don't care to know. You're just really annoying. Nobody wants you around, and that's for a pretty good reason. Don't you think Noah?" she said as a smirk appeared on her face.

"Have some respect for your daughter. I think it's best for both of us."

"I think I'm being quite reasonable in all fairness. You ruined her. Is that such a bad assumption to make?"

I didn't respond. Insecurity drove me away from the conversation. Sudden dismal thoughts provoked the strongest desire to shove her aside and run to where Leah lay. To give myself the last chance to hold her. But I didn't budge. It felt like her mother's words held me hostage, stuck to the ground I stood on. I felt strangled. I thought about how lucky I was. She was born so that I could know her. She was a good person who deserved a good life. Her mother was right in a way. About me. Always about me.

"I'm here just for her, Johanna. I lost somebody too. I deserve to grieve," I told her, with a scowl on my face.

She wasn't a real mother. She barely ever showed any care. I fucking despised her.

"Whatever Noah, do as you please. I don't want to hear from you again. I hope I make myself crystal clear."

———

42 degrees. The warm air. I felt the sun on my chest. The kitchen was wiped clean. Balmy days with wet grass. And the afterglow burnt. She came back home to me. And our skin was warm. Her face was bruised. You could see exactly which blood vessels were leaking. I didn't ask what happened. There wasn't any point in asking. I already knew the answers. It was always the same.

———

I remember sitting there, looking unphased as the time passed by. I have had many days full of blindness. This day was one of those. And she was right there, to be seen. The sun didn't shine like it usually did. I felt anxious at the idea of ending the funeral. It would act as an acceptance of her passing. I didn't want that to happen. I dreaded that happening. At least not for a very long time. I have shredded layers of flesh. The pollution inside of me is covered with rotten roots. But nothing is comparable to how pure my body was for her. I looked down. I frowned as raindrops hit the handwritten paper I was tightly holding. It created wet pools around the barely legible writing.

It read:

It is incredibly difficult to write down in words what I feel towards Leah. I wasn't quite sure of how to start it off, whether I should grieve, or be grateful for the time spent together. It's always the correct time and the correct place. That was her motto, to keep going through the hard-bitten days. To always find yourself exactly where you were. She would always tell me to just face it. Face it head-on. See what the outcome would be. Be brave, she would say. Leah was brave. Strong. Confident in her actions. She was loud. She was always there. There for you whenever you needed her. That was her. She could turn a day upside-down. Make you feel like the world needs you. Really feel it. But the world always needed you, Leah. It did. It still does. She was an angel brought to us, and she showed it throughout her time. Now I still fall in love with the memory of you, Leah. I'm enraptured with you, believe me. You deserved better. You deserved a golden throne. A place for you to bathe in undying light.

Thank you for the times spent together, and for showing me love without boundaries. Thank you for you. Thank you for creating an existence for us. In my head, I'm still dancing with you. Still dancing the evenings away. Together, hand in hand. Now I'm alone. It isn't the same. I sculpt you out of my heart. This isn't a goodbye Leah. I find that the memory of you is eternal. May heaven guide me to you.

As I read I couldn't help but think that it wasn't genuine. The words seemed to be placed without purpose. Without experience attached to it. My heart felt barren. The sentences seemed unreal. It almost created an impression that our relationship was good. It wasn't. It wasn't even close to good. I shouldn't have had to hide that, especially not from the people standing around me. *Realisation*. I walked up towards the lectern. I laid the eulogy down on the rehal. But I didn't read the words I wrote down.

"I knew her life was hanging on by a thread. It didn't come to me as a surprise when she fucking did it. But it was everything. Everything came crashing down on me. From the shitty arguments we should never have had. To the kisses we shared. Everything hit me all at once. I tried hard. I tried hard—to absorb her pain, to make sure she was okay. I now finally realise I was the mistake she invited in. But all of you know that. You make it clear. You didn't even bother to pass by. To see how she was doing. To see how I was doing. You show it by calling me in the early hours. You threaten me. You wish death on me. And while I sit up all night waiting for her to come back, you laugh. Why do you put glaring eyes upon me? Why are you so judgmental about the only thing she knew how to love? You're no better than me. Pretending you all care so much. Look at all your faces. Pathetic. But it's been clear to me. I—I was nothing. Nothing but lifeless to her. Nothing but a walking corpse. A situation she just decided to cross out one day. She cut me off cold. She left me in a war, and I'm still in that same war. But only now am I dealing with the trauma of it. I can't forgive her for that. And that hurts, you know. I waited and waited and waited for her calls. But they never came. They never did. And I couldn't understand it. I still don't. A chasm is all that's left the person I once was. I offered myself to her. All of it. I offered all of it to her. For what exactly? For her to blow her brains out all over the sidewalk. That's what she had to do to feel alive again. Shooting herself. This is not how it should have ended. I can't bear it any longer, you know? I carry this shit around with me. I carry it. I can't let it go. I try to rationalise it, to normalise it, but I can't do any of these things. The last time I saw her was with her head split open. Do you know what that— what that does to a man. Nobody should have to see that. It's trauma. It's trauma imprinted onto me. It keeps digging deeper and deeper inward until there's nothing left of me. And all of you have the fucking audacity to stand there, pushing your stupid narratives about her life. You didn't know shit! I did. You weren't there for her! I was. And why? Why did I have to love her this much. Why—fucking why! Her stories died with me! Not with all of you fucks. And where were all of you? Cause you're here now. But she doesn't need your help any more. Where were you when she used to tell me stories about coming home to you. To a house filled with nothing. And anger being every reason for the walls around her. And how you hit her. How you abused her and screamed in her ears, and pulled her hair, and locked her up. And how her father— how her father... I fucking hate you, how you touched her so violently, made her forget her worth. You made her forget who she truly could have been. I hope you're all proud of yourselves. I know for damn sure I'm not. But that's the difference, isn't it? I can admit it. I can admit the shit I brought upon her. You can't. You'll go home, back to your relief and comfort, and suck the condolences out of everybody. Is it reassuring enough to know that she won't come back to bother you? I bet it is. I bet it fucking is. You are all embarrassing. Embarrassing for Leah to be associated with. I hope you find your wrongdoings, and fix them within your damn fucked up selves. All I wanted was for her to be happy. With me. Not with anyone else. How hard is that to understand?

It should... It should have been me. It should have been me for heaven's sake."

I remember my voice starting to break as I kept crying through the ever-lasting silence. There was no compassion. There was no empathy in the room. I was the only one suffering. The offence brought by my speech hung in the expressions in front of me. Disapproval was dripping off of everyone's faces.

I try to stand up, having to use excessive force to lift myself. I sit up instead. I take some time to rest. I take off my jacket and lay it down next to me. The torn holes in my black T-shirt expose my pale skin.

'Unmendable holes,' she would say.

I always begged to differ. I always found fixes in the simplest of problems. But now, although I hate it, I have to agree. I pull at the skin folds. I get the power to stand up and make my way over to my bedside table. I start undressing as I walk.

I pick up the notebook and read yesterday's entry:

Death was waiting. It was waiting like a crow does for a rotting body. Like life does when deciding when to let you go. I fueled you with so much that it made you drown. That's the tragedy of it all. The decaying of a divinity. And I feel so wrathful. So fucking incensed at everything around me, and you. You said you were able to handle it. It's okay, it's okay, it's okay you would repeat over and fucking over again. It's not okay. It's never going to be okay.

Did it end when it needed to? Why was it supposed

to be without me? Why. Why is it that while you putrefy beneath me I do the same above? I'm surrounded by nothing but anguish and the pain of deep regret. Your image still appears everywhere I turn. I needed you, Leah, just like you needed me. Why didn't you understand that? The life you breathed into me kept me alive Leah. It kept me away from the drink. I found you twice. Twice! You never find the same person twice. I shouldn't have to eradicate every feeling of anger I experience, that doesn't come with being a better person. I can't just become a better person now that you're gone. I walk with pain as a loyal companion now, hand in hand, soul tied to soul. I was a martyr for the cause of you. The cuts are gaping. They are fathomless. They're permanent sadness.

Leah, don't take it to heart. I've fucked up as well. You know that. Stupid things only I could do. I wish I could make up for all the love you were missing, the love you thought you didn't deserve. I wish I could let your beating heart press against mine again. The world's falling apart as I pierce the silence in search of you. By the grace of God, I'm trying not to surrender to it. I am trying so fucking hard. I wonder if heaven can hold you.

A taste of pure serenity came over me today, however, seeing you get lowered down into your grave. I wanted to jump in with you, to rip my flesh off and form myself into a heap of bones at your side. I couldn't cry. Don't take it personally. I didn't have it in me, to swallow the truth and accept you gone. I wanted to break open my ribcage and free life. But at last, you are at peace, some-

where that's not this fucking hell-hole. Please forgive me, Leah. I know I can not stop death. Can you give me a sign, Leah? Please. A sign that you fucking craved me. The eternal remin—'

I can't read anything more. The rest is unclear to me. The ink is running down the page in neat lines. Almost in perfect synchronisation with each other, followed up with stains near the bottom of the page—the tears I had shed. I'm a vile being. I'm a blade that doesn't stop cutting. I'm the embodiment of a victim complex. I put the notebook back down. I'm not eager to decipher what I wrote after the blotch. My head is in complete disarray. I can't focus on a single object in the room. Everything is moving in an erratic way around me.

This can't be good, I think to myself.

But what do I expect? I'm not sleeping enough; dark, purple circles around my eyes expose the evidence. Neither am I taking any of the pills prescribed to me. I am a mess. I've always been a subtle kind of fucked-up mess. But words can't express how I love to bathe in the mess. I think it will be good to keep silent for a while.

I chew her up, then spit her out. Then I wonder why I still want her.

———

My surroundings are starting to spin, and I feel another blackout coming. But this time it doesn't. It's the unwillingness to bear the load of life left behind. The image of the pathologist's blade closely inspecting Leah's body up and down. A clinical autopsy to reveal her most grisly secrets. To expose her inner being out to the open air. For people to judge. For people to form a biased fucking opinion about. Buried in a bottomless pit. Covered with the earth's dirt to be dug up again as nothing but lifeless remains. I sit on the bed. I think about what to do. I decide to lie down and listen to the street's silence below. Not many people are around this morning. A few more than yesterday. The day is bright and sunny. Full of sentience. But I'm not. Of course I'm not. It's hard to wait around for something to happen. Hopefully something bad. It kills me. I decide to take a look outside. Peering over the rooftops I can just about make out the synagogue a few streets down. I feel grounded whenever I take a moment to rest. It relieves me. I pull a fresh unopened cigarette pack from the bedside table. I take one out and light it up. I exhale, and keep exhaling until my lungs are empty. Smoke renews the air around me. I cough. I normally never open the windows. I like the seductive smell of it. The warm, complex undertones possess me as the residual odour clings to the objects in the room. The tobacco is slowly burning away. The orange ring shines mildly, eating away at the paper. I smoke because it reminds me of the taste of her breath. I like losing myself to a different taste. *Instead of the ones I am already used to.* I feel an absence of anger. And I find myself lost in bad faith. I tap the cigarette against the ashtray, closely feeling the nicotine releasing the adrenaline. It causes me to suddenly jolt up.

I'll visit the bar downstairs, I think.

I start putting my clothes on while I thirst for a drink.

The bar isn't much. The door is nearly off its handles. It opens with difficulty. It has a broken wooden frame. Attached to the door, with nothing but a piece of tape, is a dirty sign that says 'always open'. The floorboards creak when I take the first step inside. It reeks of sweat. The repelling odour of wet dog enters my nose. It is a quiet afternoon. Nothing much is happening in the worn-down interior. It looks like it's on life support. It for sure is. Only a couple of men are sitting on bar stools, drinking away at whatever poison they choose. I don't know why I came here, it makes it more difficult to stay sober. But it was our favourite place. I feel animosity towards it. It'll do. It used to be a place where time stood still. Where subtle acts of love were offered. Placing my hand on hers. We would hold each other until we got sweaty.

'Fuck it, right?' I think to myself.

What's the point of being sober if it doesn't even help? I might as well take a drink to swallow away any of the remaining pride I have left. There is no audience. There is no approval needed. There is nobody to disappoint with it all. I am no longer tied to my sobriety. I no longer have to convince myself to believe I can be a better person. Or to be awarded with mournful applause. God, I am naive. All of this has once again led me to the place I needed to get away from. I wonder if I will ever stop wallowing in the pleasure of drinking for longer than a fucking week. I should have never come here. *I never even said sorry.* Apologies were seemingly always forced by Leah. I found myself pleading at her side at every chance I got. For any ounce of forgiveness. I begged and begged for her to stay. It only led me to drink more. I wanted so badly to forget how much I hated her. And when she would make herself believe in my promises and apologies, I would strip them away from her the very next chance I got. I wish I hadn't. But there is no longer a reason to hope. The remains of what could have been done are now found back in the alcohol.

All I desperately find myself wanting is to drink it away. There is no point arguing against what I crave. The addiction will still always come out on top, no matter what. It strips me naked. It fucks you up so badly. You start to hate yourself without it. It sacrifices unborn problems. I couldn't see a clear enough way out of it anymore. Thoughtless intakes of venom brought life back into my blood and reanimated me with the man I thought I always knew to be. I would use the alcohol to fuel the burning of my decaying life. But nobody ever noticed the smoke rising from out of me, until she came along and noticed it right away. There was nothing more I needed than the veracity of the day, and any less would have done me a disfavour. I would not have considered drinking any longer. I do not think I ask for much. You either give in to it, or you don't ever get to again. That is the duality you face. The lies are found within me, trapped within the sadness that I borrow from the world. It's a lending hand. The bartender walks over.

"Can I get a Sazerac?" I ask the bartender.

"Do you want it with Rye or cognac?" he politely asks back.

"Uh, just add both."

I know Leah wouldn't approve, but I need to feel another sensation other than the anguish. It takes me away to a false reality. A place where ungratefulness wouldn't have led me astray. Somewhere I don't have to be subjected to being berated by people I call close. Somewhere before I got fucked up. When coughing up blood in public bathrooms was my biggest worry. When the silence wasn't too much to handle. I used to be drunk and sentimental. I have a longing that's killing me. And I have done nothing with being alive. I glance over and see the bartender walk towards me.

"Here you go. A Sazerac," he says loudly, placing it on a little beige tissue.

"Thanks," I reply.

And here we are. I'm back at a bar, drinking. As I take the first, bitter sip I can feel my heart struggle for air. The alcohol burns on my tongue. I live for the taste. I let it sit in my mouth for one second more. I let the bile creep up my throat. Then I don't, and I force it down. I let it go straight to my head. And tomorrow I will do it again. And again. I'll never know restraint the way I should. But I am glad I still have a heart.

Oh well, I think.

'I'll just hope for March's better days.'

Why doesn't your absence bother you, Noah?

Chapter 2
Bare My Teeth To Show What Consumes Me

It is now the following year, May. Spring is coming to its terminal end. The gentle warmth is halting its journey, and the fierce, fiery hotness of the summer is approaching.

I haven't gotten better. The bruises continue to ache. But I am now in a search—in search of something more. Something I can share with open blessings. There are still plenty of days that feel meaningless, with long nights consumed by grievances. I feel more among the living now. But the pain no longer retracts itself from my body. The alcohol is as strong as ever, and I am realising change is not a simple option. My blood thirsts for it. But I was never good at coping—with anything. I barely remember things. At least not in detail. And I need God to visit me again.

Try to drink me away and I'll try to let myself be drunk. All for you.

I'm sitting overlooking the lake. Reflections are lightly bouncing off the surface. I think about Mama. I think about how she would tell me that people treat you exactly how they feel about you, so I shouldn't be so blind, and how she drudged so silently throughout her miserable life. Papa died young. Overnight. Suddenly. It caught us all by surprise. He wasn't a good father. Nor a decent husband. He would come home late at night, barge in to yell at Mama, beat on her and decide she was no good for him any more. Mama wouldn't bother. She was used to the treatment. I would scream and shout and lose myself in defense of her, but she was too scared to leave.

The house became cold for a long while. Then, after his passing, it grew warm. We became happy—at his expense. She would beg me sometimes. Beg me not to become my papa. Not to lose the person I was. But I did somehow. *Will you keep calling me? I worry about you now that you're grown.*

I neglected her. I would get angry at seeing her decay. I would act out of frustration instead of empathy. The pain a mother should never have to feel. I abandoned her. Mama's small, fine lips would curve to the side when she smiled, up to her dark pupils. They would enlarge at the sight of me. Her end couldn't have come quick enough. Clear as day, she was in deep torment. Everybody knew it. She didn't want to speak about it. Because she couldn't. Simple actions had become laborious and her speech would turn into a confused mess. It was a struggle, not because she kept forgetting, but because she didn't realise she was. Memories became insignificant time capsules. The world around us kept moving at a pace she couldn't keep up with. Bygone days being burned away. And I would be covered in the soot. There was no clear avenue. A hymn lost in translation. The disease kept eating away at her. It nibbled at every chance it got until there was nothing left. Nothing at all. A body without a soul. A clock without time. A wedding without a veil. And that was her end. A blank canvas. To live your last moments in ignorance is probably the best way to go about it. To let life engulf you. Chasing fleeting moments, only to find yourself at death's door. Dying peacefully is a privilege not everybody can afford. She couldn't. She lost her life two times. Once mine. Once hers.

I desire her peace. Nobody teaches you how to take care of your own mama. It wouldn't do any damage to ask God for help. I yearn for her. I yearn for her.

I feel urgency stalk me. I touch the ground beneath me for a sense of unity. I feel my organs contract with whatever I have left within me. I feel them pleading for another drink. I grab the silver hip flask from my pocket. I engraved it with Mama's initials. It never stops me. Bruised and bloodied I lie down. I am barely holding on to my sense of consciousness. I nurse the remnants of sharp pain with a bitter sip. The birds turn and whirl in hopeful murmurations around the white puffy clouds. The sky is blue. Bluer than I've ever seen. I've redialed Leah plenty of times. Her voicemail. To hear her voice speak words. To decipher each word as if it were my own mouth speaking them. Some people never leave your bones. You carry them around like marrow. I stand up, carefully spinning the bottle cap back on the flask. It's getting late. The north wind is starting to slither in through my messy curls. I make my way back to the car. It is all I own, except for the apartment of course. It's an old thing. The side mirrors are a mess of shards. The front window is filled with cracks. There are scratches on all of its corners. It's nothing special, but to me, it is. Cause it's mine. I open the door with little to no force and I sit inside. I let out a hefty yawn. I take the usual road to get back home. It isn't far if I can escape the usual 6 p.m. traffic.

Where I unfold, I am true. And that always seems to happen when I'm around you.

It carries no importance now. The sun is disappearing behind the mountains to the left of me. The bright orange hues wane into the sky as I slowly breathe in and out. It thumps. Up and down. The grass sways to the right, steering away from the turbulent noise created by the cars rushing past. I rotate the crank handle situated under my window, letting the humid air take up the remaining space. I reach for my flask again. I twist the top off and take heavy draughts of its contents. The road ahead no longer seems straight. It bends in all directions. I realise I am driving in circles. Blind-sighted. I'm losing my way at every curve.

"Noah what the actual fuck are you doing," I sarcastically say.

I'm not completely present. I turn the radio on to be met with loud static. I switch the channels around. I try to find something that appeases me. I cycle through whatever signals it grabs. But there's nothing. There's only the usual political issues, all based on the usual self-informed opinions.

"And that's enough," I say, pressing the button to release the radio unit from its dock.

I reach over to place it in the glove box.

I see the city come into full view. It doesn't bother me, but I don't necessarily like the fakeness of it all. The man-made concrete jungle. Always expanding to take us all. I am located further away, past the city, up on top of the hill where privacy can exist fundamentally. Where people can rest away from prying eyes. The city has viability though. I am not really into that. I rather be constrained to the essence of being real and credible. You know, a human that is not enslaved to any sort of work mentality. Or maybe that is just laziness talking. Whatever it is, the drive doesn't take long, as I had already suspected. And as I park my car I see Elias walk along the pathway. I decide to visit him later. Maybe have a drink. It might do us both some good.

———

I knock on his door. Three hard knocks. It is now 7:47 p.m. By now I would be flat-out drunk. But not today. I haven't gone out in a long while, always comforting myself with the fact I wouldn't have to. Today I did. It felt kinda nice. Just nice. But that's okay. It's something to occupy my mind with, to know things are still out there. I don't have to conform to the self-made rule of staying locked up in the apartment. Elias finally opens the door. About time.

"Oh, Noah. What are you doing here?" he hastily says.

"I thought it would be good to talk. About things."

There is no immediate answer. Maybe this was not the best idea. Opening up practically to a stranger was not what I needed right now. For some reason something was telling me to go through with it.

"Or I could come back another time if I'm bothering you Elias?"

Fuck. Had he forgotten what he said last week? I feel like such an asshole showing up like this. Am I putting myself into his personal business?

"No, absolutely not. Please, come in. Make yourself at home," Elias responds.

I enter his homely apartment. There isn't much

difference to mine, except for the fact this one is clean. Very clean. I notice the books spread out across the floor. Some are torn. Some are in pristine condition. I walk close behind him. I follow as his shadow. I don't want to feel like I'm intruding into his house. We get to the living area and there isn't a lot to see.

"Sorry for the mess Noah," Elias nervously says.

He quickly throws things off the table. A random assortment of items scatter on the ground. Elias doesn't seem to make any attempt to pick anything back up. Now the only area in the house which is unclean lies directly in front of me on the burgundy-coloured Persian carpet. It's a heap of what seems to be newspapers, pens and a gold spoon. I look at Elias once again. Confusion builds on my face.

"Yeah, sorry."

"Don't be sorry man. You alright?" I laughingly ask.

"I don't know. Is it too warm? As in, the temperature? Is it?" Elias sputters out, hesitating at every word.

He pulls up his shirt sleeve. Then I spot it, the immense track marks on his arms. The blunt needles on the floor. They're leaking out tar-coloured liquid. I piece everything together. The immediate moral culpability overtakes me. I see myself as the main issue in the situation. Sickness rises. My body grows weaker by the second. My eyes widen at the sight. I am a traitor. A traitor to every relationship I built. From the very foundation to the essence of my being. A traitor to my closest surroundings. To the people who offer me the help that they fucking need themselves. *Repressed.* I know exactly why Elias is doing this. I know why he has these substances in his system. The thought is lingering at the tip of my tongue. My face turns pale at the thought of it. It loses all its previous colour. I stagger back. I look at

Elias, who hasn't seen my face yet. His eyes are too ashamed to meet mine.

"Leah sold it to me Noah," he shakingly says.

I know he's right. I pretend not to believe him. I turn around and rush outside, not knowing exactly what to do. I walk downstairs forcefully, avoiding Elias's calls from upstairs. I enter my apartment. I shut the door behind me and I lean against it for support. My destructive tendencies catch up to me. I can hear Elias's cries upstairs. He's pleading. Pleading for God to save him. It breaks me. It breaks me to hear him tear his lungs apart. It's exhausting. He starves and doesn't talk. He uses and uses and uses and he still doesn't talk. He never says anything at all. I fall to my knees in an act of despair, knowing I am witness to another ruination. Tears overflow the place I once called home. I start to drown. A deluge circulates me. There is no good reason for the water to split apart. I look at the veins bulge out of my sweat-covered skin. The blood pulses through every pipe. The tendons appear stiff, causing me to barely be able to move any part of my body. I lift my hands in front of me. They are shaking aggressively as if they are trapped under the thick meat binding them. They want to be free. I feel the slaughter of my psyche. Its intricate layers are agonisingly scraped off with immense force. As I try to calm myself, I reach out for any other thought that shoots across. It doesn't work. Pain oozes over me as I reflect on what I saw upstairs. The deterioration of Elias. A ceiling in between us, with nothing to break it. How could I let this fucking happen? I let everything happen. My eyes are burning with repentance. The image of myself no longer subsists. Cause after cause. Shame after shame. I can finally connect the dots. I can finally trace myself back to all the horrors I am bridged to. I reach for my back pocket, trying to find the lighter I always carry.

I have to calm myself. My fingers search around in the pocket as I panic. I can't fucking find it. I check my back pocket, and this time I do. I find it tucked deep inside. I grab it neurotically and flick it on.

"Please. Please turn on," I say.

The flame comes on. I hold it close to my arm. Against it. It takes me back to when we would scald each other's skin. Like a tattoo. With more delicacy. My arm is covered with these scars. A collection of moments that showed reverence to life as it is. It's the abuse that you face that binds you to who you are. I notice myself staring at the shattered mirror. Caught in the reflection I start to plaintively weep again. I'm no longer pitiable. I do this to myself. The migraine comes back as if I was not expecting it to. My eyes roll back into my skull. With the whites exposed, I fall strongly on my right side.

I find myself spiralling into dreams. Moments come flashing by as if I've never been confronted with them. I find myself in a room. All the lights are off. But people are watching and listening in the far reach of darkness. I know what this is. This was my second rehab meeting. The one I had after Leah's passing. I can feel my heart pump blood faster than it has ever done before. This is a recurring dream; I've had it before and it's never great. I find myself repeating what I said that day:

"Hey everyone. You all probably know me by now. Uh, where... where do I start. As you know I'm an alcoholic, and my girlfriend's an alcoholic too, was an alcoholic too, sorry, and well... uh... that's why I'm here. Things tend to move very fast because she... well she passed away around a week ago and I'm here because truthfully I don't really have anyone to talk to, so I thought this was or would be the perfect outlet. I don't think there's anything inherently wrong with me but... I'm not sure, there— there might be you know. Something is broken within me because I feel it. I feel it... anyways, uh... where was I getting at? The truth. Right. The truth is vital, as we all know, and—uh—it's that, that it's not easy for me to live without constantly having to portray myself as a casualty in the midst of it all because I'm simply not, I mean, I'm not and... and I've never wanted to be this and I'm dealing with all of this fucking... this shit up here in my head, all alone, always. I just can't... can't shake the image of her out of my damn mind. I didn't know she was on the verge of doing it. I didn't. And... and her drinking it just all happened so fast right in front of me and I didn't notice because— because I was so, so blind to myself. I was blind to myself. How could my eyes be open to her? I—It couldn't have been, could it? And I was there for her when she needed me, you know, I was. Her family was hurting her, bad, real bad and I was there when she needed me, just not all the time you get it? I would work long shifts and she would disappear for days, and I didn't see it as a call for help. I saw it as retribution. Maybe—Maybe I had done something to upset her, you know? Maybe it was a part of who she was as a person, I didn't understand it. But now I do. Now I do, but it's too late for me to change anything, to travel back in time. And then when she left, a couple of days before her—her passing, I contained it all within myself. I didn't deem her bad, or, or go running after her. She knew what she wanted, and I accepted it wholeheartedly. I was fucking postponing my feelings in case she came back. Back to me. I held back, with purpose. I finally had a purpose. To change who I was in case she came back. For the first time, I felt purpose within me. And I knew—I knew my wrongdoings and all the shit I had done to her... I finally fucking understood what she needed, what she wanted. Help. It was just help and love and pain and emotion. It was her way of communicating, to drink and drink and drink. She made that her purpose. To be one with the person she was that she had tried so hard to resemble. To resemble me, because I liked her more when she was high, or drunk, when we were open to each other, and stopped keeping doors closed—locked from one another and it broke us and—fuck! It broke us to pointless pieces, and there was no way to mend it. There wasn't an easy way out, but she fucking found it didn't she? And it still was unexpected. We kissed with morning breath, we kissed when we were sick, we kissed when we were mad and we weren't supposed to go anywhere. But I couldn't fix it. I couldn't fucking fix it and I feel fucked up. And I can't even be grateful that I'm alive because the day she died, a part of me died too, you know? I didn't mean to be bad. I swear I am an okay person. I have it within me. Somewhere. Someplace safe. I am okay. I am okay."

I looked around the room. Inside me something seethed.

"Uh—Thank you. Thank you guys for letting me share"

I wake up in the same foetal position I was in. I am still in front of the door, in the narrow dimly lit hallway. A light touch of a stranger's hand is placed on my shoulder, brushing it slowly from front to back. It creates a comfortable friction I have not felt in a while. I can't make out who it is. I recognise the smell. I open my eyes to intense physical pain from behind their sockets. My eyesight is still blurred. All I can make out is a figure on his knees beside me.

"How did you get in here? Who the fuck..." I say.

I have difficulty with vocalising my words. The figure doesn't answer. It steps back slowly so as not to make itself known.

"Sorry, Noah. I couldn't help but come check up on you," the figure says.

I immediately recognise the careful voice. I gave him a copy of my keys. In case.

"Elias, I'm okay," I answer back softly.

"I can see that."

What do I even say? No explanation is needed. Out of all people he would surely understand. Would he? Even after having never once checked up on him, while he cried nights away? Or when I would see him standing out alone. I choose to ignore his signs of alienation. How would an explanation not be necessary? A man without the strength to own up to his own mistakes. Of course I needed to talk to Elias, to ask how he was doing. I needed to help him get rid of this disturbing dependency. But was that up for me to decide? To decide whether somebody should stop the oxygen they inhale. To decide if life is not painful enough to end. No, it isn't up to me. I know for damn sure I won't help him. I have my shit. And he has his. I am pleading for it to stay that way.

"Noah, I didn't know you were coming, I would have hidden it away, I didn't know. Please forgive me. It isn't easy for me either. I've had—"

I cut him off.

"Elias. Keep your problems to yourself. I've lost it too, can't you see?"

"Come on. I'm really trying here."

"I can't fucking help you like I did last year. You

continued. That's on you, man. That's on you this time. Decisions don't just fall into another person's lap. Deal with it for fuck's sake. And don't bother—"

"I need help. Please Noah," Elias says.

"Did you not hear me, Elias? Listen to the fucking words. I don't like you. I don't know you. I don't want you around. I don't give a shit what you do. Disappear for all I care. You should realise this shit won't make you feel good, okay? Take that as a solid piece of advice."

"The doctors said I don't have that long left Noah. It's starting to really eat me up," he says.

He's afraid to walk alone. This is his tragedy. This is what has been picked out by hand for him by whichever angels select our destinies from the shelves of possible lives. But he doesn't understand this yet. Not yet. Maybe he will. *He cannot let go.*

"Why are you telling me all this? Waste yourself away and you'll only have yourself to thank."

I immediately regret everything, from going up to his apartment to talk, to degrading him when he asks for some decency. Elias takes a final look at me. He lets his hand go. He turns around and heads towards the open door. He stumbles away, imprecise and hesitant. He makes his way up the set of stairs.

"Hey, Elias. Look I'm sorry, okay? Elias!" I shout, praying he will take notice.

But he doesn't. *I'll feel it when he's gone.* He doesn't even turn around to acknowledge it. He just keeps walking up until he simply vanishes out of sight. I don't hasten either. I don't even bother to follow him up there. I slowly stand up, leaning against the brittle wall for some support. I am no good here. I need to find a way out. I need to find a retreat from all the shit I bring upon this place. I pace back and forth, accusing myself of things that haven't even happened. I'm thinking dangerous thoughts. The idea of leaving everything grim behind makes we want to hide between the skeletons in my closet. I think and think and think until there is no more thinking left to do. And then I think some fucking more about fucking thinking. I put my hand in my jeans, searching around for a cigarette. No luck. I drag myself to the bedroom. I guide myself over to my bedside table and open the top drawer. I use too much force. The drawer comes dangling out. Idiot. I scuffle around until I find around half a dozen cigarettes hidden at the back. I grab one and ignite it as I put another one behind my ear. It's true what they say. A place is only as good as the people. And this place sucks. It sucks bad. Uncertainty instils fear in me. Where would I even find myself at? There is nothing around here. I have to go far. That would be damn far. But perhaps that's not bad. Not bad to think about getting away from here.

I open my closet and frantically throw everything out on the floor. There's not much to throw. To the ordinary person, it would seem like a collection of rags. The disorganised mess provokes liveliness. I am keeping a stiff backbone against the clear conscience I'm battling with. I don't want to leave this place. In truth I know I should. I see my bag under the bed. I grab it. I unzip it and begin pushing as much as I can inside. Scuffling through the clothes my eyes fall upon a pair of lace underwear. I pick it up. I'm sure she left this on purpose. I can't risk carrying more baggage than I already have, and the various assortment of items laid in front of me bring me sadness. Bringing it with me would bring the apartment with it. I can't afford that any longer. I can't continuously live with the past holding me back. I have to repress my emotions. I don't want to be a prisoner in my head. But I already am. There isn't much left to take with me. The room grows colder with it. A house that is no longer a home. The night sky peers through the curtains. It illuminates the walls with bluish hues. There could have been paradise. But all that is left is just what is left. The bed still stands in the same place but without clothes covering the sheets. The table's foot is still loose, probably looser than when I first kicked it, and the couch is still in need of replacement. But it's over now. There isn't going to be any change any more. Not here. I put my ear to the wall, pressing it against the rugged surface. I hear Leah calling out to me from the inside. She's pleading with me to not leave. Her voice is muffled, as if she is inside, stuck behind the concrete and brick. She's yelling, digging away at the walls to get to where I'm standing. I hear her voice become unnerved. Her nails break as she attempts to dig. I feel chills run along my spine as sinister words erupt from the walls, surrounding me. I step back. I try to catch my breath again. I find myself in dejection. I don't want to suffer any more. Her voice was the blood that streams to my heart. The mind that controls me. She needs me to stay here. But I can't give in to that. Not any more. I can't do it any more. I start hitting myself. Out of pure anger. I feel like I'm punishing myself every second that goes by. The longer I stay, the more longing I have to stay. Tomorrow was never promised to me. Neither was it to Leah. That's exactly why I have to go. I have to make it a promise well kept. I grab my flask and as I put my mouth on it I realise it's completely empty. I turn it around and shake it aggressively. Nothing comes out.

"Fuck, man," I say.

I desperately look around, lusting for alcohol to surrender to. The drinking is wasting me away. It traps me in a state of psychosis. But I really need this. I find a Smirnoff bottle, hidden under the bathroom sink. Thank God I have a reserve. I take off the cap and swallow as much down as possible. The burn rushes through me. But I like it. It acts as a cure. It's easier to be angry at the world than at yourself. To ignore the duty of dealing with fucking everything bad happening around you. To put blame on your sadness. It is a cathartic release.

As I close the door behind me I take a last look at the sombre remains of the apartment. I feel shame. Why couldn't I have left when Leah did, and why could I not open up to my cowardice before? I reach the stairs, and I stay standing for a while. I'm not sure if I should say goodbye to Elias. I don't think I deserve to do so, and for Elias it just wouldn't be a good reminder of the events today. Besides, it was late, and I probably wouldn't find him in the best mood either. I walk down, ignoring the urge to stay. At the bottom, the steps extend towards the exit through a narrow hallway. I run my hands along the stair railing, embracing the stone-cold touch pulse through my fingers. As I walk closer it seems like the exit goes back further, and further. I start walking quicker, erasing all doubts of leaving this place behind me. I raise my hand forward, reaching out towards the door, and without warning, it appears directly in front of me. And it connects hard. I push through as the door destructively hits the side of the building. I'm outside again in the warm evening breeze. The heat takes over my whole body. The cosy glow of the streetlights light up the subtle pools of water stuck in the crevices of the road, and I take my first step into the unknown journey ahead of me.

I get to the parked car and take a long pause before entering. There is a weightless presence. Without burden attached to it. I hold onto my chest as I feel it surge within me. It's healing broken bones and vicious scars. I pray with penetrable eyes. Leah has sent me a sign. I know what she is trying to communicate. That it's okay. Okay for me to choose myself. That it is okay to try to let go. To let go of the dense mist I always find myself lost in. To let go of mournful feelings. To replace them with the existence of hope. To find hope for my very own, and to clutch it. To never let go of what is right. I step into the car. For the very first time, there is quiet solitude. The voices in my head no longer strike my temper, but they drift around each other. I am no longer alone. I can find pieces of myself within the splintered fragments of memory, and Leah is there for brief moments, falling in and out of thought. I hold up my hand to await Leah's hand, but she isn't there physically. There's silence. I see Leah's ghost sitting next to me. Although it hurts, I don't try to keep her there. I try to let go.

―――

You would have erased yourself. The hornets she left kept stinging me. The pistol was wrapped in plastic. It was given to me for my protection. I didn't want it. I didn't fucking want it. But it was given. She got it off some shady guy. He had trafficked a whole load of firearms. She said I needed it. And that I would be thankful for it. She had one too. That didn't make it any better. She was the one selling. It wasn't me. She didn't even make that much money doing it. Only on good days was it worth it. Her thumbs would be sore and her fingertips black from counting all of it up. The whole building was buying from her. I had trouble helping. I felt guilty. Not everyone actually wants to buy. In fact, they need to. They think they need it more than they need their own liver or lungs. They depend on it. Their mouths were filled with cavities, and their gums were almost grey. They would want even more when it was laced. Their cracked lips couldn't wait to ask. She tried to justify it. She said the government did the same. They sold alcohol, prescription pills and tobacco. It wasn't the same. It never was. But she dealt with it. She dealt with it better than I ever could. She would try the samples. She couldn't overcome that. She stopped touching me the same. She said it was only for a minute at a time. I didn't know what she meant. I never stopped feeling her. I pretended when she was gone. And when she was back. I was able to get her out of it. But she moved onto something else.

I check the gas meter. Nearly empty. Enough to last around a couple of hours. I turn on the ignition. I back up out of the parking space. I don't have a plan, or a route to follow. All I know is that a new beginning is definitely necessary. I am going to grab the opportunity by the fucking balls. No more delaying, or searching for something that will never appear. I have to put my foot down, and no longer surrender to the idea of what could have been. I drive along the thin stretches of road, curving down the mountain in a zig-zag pattern, past the oak trees lined up against both sides. The synagogue comes up to the left of me. A temple of healing upon a consecrated land. I remember days I prayed. Day after day. I tried harvesting will. I see the apartment fade into the distance.

Chapter 3
Bones & Tissues

I'm driving for around an hour and forty-five minutes. There is a lot I've witnessed. New sites line the way forwards. The stars light the view around me up. There's barely any traffic tonight. Headlights hit my windshield. I stare at the rearview mirror. *The other sun reflects against the barrel.* I remember that I have to find a petrol station. As a kid, I always wanted to venture out. There was no understanding. There were no harsh injuries or defacement. It was a time when scars had contentment. When bleeding was scary and new. A situation where your teeth would fall out, and you would put them under your pillow. The lamp-lit rooms, filled with family aggression and recognition. When different versions of the same song being sung to make me sleep wouldn't get boring. Feeble mind. Mama gave me a childhood. A real childhood. And I didn't make her proud. That's the worst of it all. She gave me heaven on earth. I took it for granted. I remember acting bad sometimes, shouting and kicking at the care she so carefully gave me. I reach for the bag behind me on the back seat. Without any eyes on the road I search for the half-empty Smirnoff bottle. I shouldn't drink right now, but what damage would it do to take a sip.

You're so far gone.

We were friends first. Before anything. She had a boyfriend. I didn't like him but she did. He took us out for dinner once. It was nice of him to include me.

"I'm gonna freshen up in the bathroom."

"Babe? Again?" he said.

He had thin eyebrows. A scar lined the side of his mouth.

"Uh-huh"

Leah stood up and left. He leaned in closer to me.

"Listen man. You gotta do me a favour."

His eyes kept darting over to the door in the corner. The one she went through.

"What's up?" I asked.

"You gotta tell me what she's up to. I don't trust her. Is she trying with you?"

"No man. She's just a friend."

"I caught her trying before. She's a fucking whore when she wants to be."

He rubbed his face. Then he scratched his head. He seemed unclean. I dropped my cutlery. It made a ringing sound on the plate.

"Yeah. I don't play with that shit either. But don't call her a whore, all right?"

"Excuse me?" he said.

"Don't call her a whore. You heard me."

He seemed offended. I didn't give a shit. He leaned back into the couch. He didn't say much for the rest of the night. But he was right not to trust her. Exactly fourteen minutes later we were both in the bathroom. Her nails scratched the back of my head.

I need to find a place to park for a while. My thoughts are running wild. I have no idea where I am. That's okay. I unintentionally rest my eyes on a sign in the distance that says there is service in the next three kilometres. I start driving to the right lane, indicating I'm going to get off soon. After a few seconds I see the exit I have to take. I reach a small town. It doesn't seem much bigger than the one I left behind. Cramped boxy houses fill the roads to each side. I make sharp turns, occasionally throwing me off balance. There are people walking around. As they walk they give each other dirty looks. The town seems poverty-stricken. The wearisome greyness of it all feels dense. There are large towers everywhere you look. Smoke and mist combine in the air. I drive further and I finally reach the service station I was searching for. I step outside, and the smell of benzene punctures my lungs. It makes me cough, but I don't mind the gasoline-like aroma of it. Nobody else is around. Some abandoned cars are parked to the left side, and the pumps look outdated. Silent noise hits my eardrums. My body feels on edge for some reason. Something doesn't feel right. I've had this feeling a lot recently. *I've planned my demise. I've seen it happen.* The sterile condition of the gas station shares a corresponding ambience to the hospital I often visited.

Her grave will fit her better than her landlocked home.

Mama wasn't fond of it. She clearly wanted to show that. They cramped her into a small, lightless room, and that was the end of it. That was the end of her life. She laid there for weeks, suffering through the days, and counting the minutes as they passed. There wasn't anything I could have done, except watch her slowly perish. Sometimes the golden hues of outside would filter through the window. I would drag her bed closer to the window to let it hit her face. This never failed to make her smile. She would close her eyes and her wrinkles smiled alongside her. I'm starting to forget how they formed. Or how her laugh sounded. Maybe her end was part of the butterfly effect of having me. Why did Mama have to birth me. If only I was never there, or here, and she could take time to properly live. To live for herself. To tread without fear. To find out she could love herself more than she ever thought possible. Why did she fucking decide to have me? I would rather not have existed, and not have slaved her to a purpose other than taking care of herself. A different life. She wouldn't have been subject to the mistreatment of Papa, or the endless and countless times she would be dismissed completely. She would have been in pursuit of her dreams. She wouldn't have given it up to make me feel like I could have dreams of my own. I didn't do anything with them anyways. It crushes me.

The world somehow feels like it isn't spinning anymore. I try ignoring it. As I fill up the tank I carefully keep my eyes on the flicking figures. I don't have a lot of money. My previous jobs never paid me well, but I had enough saved up in case. I would always get fired. I had to hop from job to job. I had to find a suitable spot that allowed my work ethic. The tank is nearly half-way full. I don't let it go any further. I tap it inside and I close the fuel door. I then walk inside the service station. I see Leah, standing in the aisle next to me. I feel my stomach twist and turn, as cold sweat begins to devour me alive. Her wavy black hair falls on her shoulders, and her eyes grow big at the sight of me. Small lines are created around her green irises. Her thin, slender hands reach out to me. They open to invite me in.

"Baby? Leah?"

Pretending is all that I have left now. I wish she could see me, doing something. Accepting life as it's supposed to be. Living it as she would have wanted me to. Her constant presence fulfils my grief. It's unwounded appearance makes me live in constant tension. I hate it. It never followed a regular pattern. It always shows up when I least expect it to. I don't know what comes next. I feel ashamed by it, but I don't let it overtake me. This isn't the first time I've seen Leah's ghost. My head falls forward, and I continue looking for a till to pay. The interior of the station feels dirty. Products are scattered everywhere around me, and nothing is in the correct order. Food packets lie crushed under my feet. I realise my hallucinatory encounter might have been the cause of the mess.

"Shitty place anyways," I mumble under my breath as I bend down to pick up the items from the floor.

The industrialised hanging lights nearly blind me as I walk over to the alcohol. It gives me a painful sensation behind my eyes. There are so many options, all lined up neatly. Bottle after bottle. Choice after choice. *You're the burning man*. Choosing one is difficult, but I don't care. It just practically insinuates that I will take a couple. I fill my arms and hands with whatever seems best and I go to pay.

"Uh," I say.

I dig around in my back pocket for cash.

"—number... number seven."

"Alright."

He types something into the machine.

"That'll be 27 for the gasoline, plus... uhm," the worker says, shocked at the amount of alcohol I'm buying. The shame of being seen consumes me. But he doesn't seem judgemental. He seems extremely sorry for me. I have become good at distinguishing the differences between them. Sympathy gets drawn from weakness. I'd rather have judgement thrown at me. It nourishes the desires to change. It deflects the frustration of agreement. If they knew what I had to go through they wouldn't show any consolation. They don't understand. They've never been through it. This isn't the first time. It for sure won't be the last. But I am used to the distaste at the sight of my addiction. I breed it and give it spiteful growth. My attachment towards it messes me up. It puts in place perceivances of resentment, even when it's not in plain sight. The truth is always clear, no matter how hard a person hides it. They can see it. It's written on your damn forehead.

"That's 87 total."

I pull out all the cash I have. I start straightening the wrinkled notes out. I count what I have and give it to him.

"That's not enough."

"It's all I have."

"I can't do anything with this. You have to pay the full amount."

I search around in all of my pockets, flipping them inside out. I wish I could just pull out a gun. Run out without paying anything. Pistol whip him. Maybe leave him with a bleeding nose. I realise I have some money in the car.

"I have the rest in the car."

"We're closing soon," he says, seemingly annoyed.

"Okay. Wait a minute and I'll be right back with your money."

He nods as I place the items on the cash desk. I rush to the car, where I reach into the glovebox. I rummage around. I find an old picture. It's a picture of me and Leah, and the car. Back when I bought it. I was so happy with it. We were happy with it. I hold the photo between my fingers. I zone out. Nausea clouds me. Why do I always have to be reminded. I need to leave it behind. Flies and other insects swarm around me. They buzz. They're attracted to the light. I come back to my senses and I grab some cash. Barely enough. I get back and give him the money.

"Thank you, have a safe drive."

I walk to the door as a bell exclaims my departure. I can finally smell the outside air again. I get to my car. I open the booth and drop the bottles inside. I step inside and sit back for a brief moment. I am barely holding on to staying awake. My face feels sore, and there is a foggy blur enclosing me. I rub my hands against my face viciously, and I sit up, not allowing myself to slouch. I open the glovebox and grab a supply of paracetamol. I grab two pills and swallow them directly down. Things around me are starting to fade in and out. I rest my head backwards against the headrest, trying to maintain my left-over sanity. However, I carry on. I drive out of the town the same way I came. I feel some relief that it's over with. Social interactions don't go hand in hand with me. It is too late to be dealing with anything more for today.

It's innately valuable. It will hit like waves.

Day and night collide. They entrance each other. The soft hills wave over the horizon. The rising sun casts a red glow over it all. It's early morning. I have to find a place to rest soon. The road stretches out ahead of me, far into the blank. And there doesn't seem to be any end to it. I feel helpless, and disorientated, fatigue taking over me. I clutch harder on the wheel, trying to find some equilibrium. I attempt to roll down my window. But I physically can't.

I held her tight to me. She was having a panic attack. She had a lot of them. They would bring her to tears. It came in sheep's skin. It was revealed as pure fear.

"I can't get it out of my mind any more."

She was lying against me. She had nowhere else to be.

"It hurts, Noah. It fucking hurts."

I caress her hair. It's soft just like she is.

"His hands still touch me. And I ask him not but he always does."

I hope it can rest gently on her shoulders.

I pull up to the side of the road. I stumble out of the car, throwing up all over the ground beneath me. The acidic taste mixes with the saliva as I spit in an attempt to get rid of any remaining vomit. I feel bleached. A terrible pain rises to my head. I hold onto it, violently.

"Oh, fuck." I say.

I'm all alone, standing here. The car is parked on a slanted part of the road. I sigh. I decide to take a piss. I zip open my jeans and I let out all of the alcohol. I can barely piss straight. It takes some effort but I get it done. I hold onto the roof of the car, paying attention to my surroundings. There is a small stream running alongside me. It leads into the forest. The trees stand big. They tower above me. Nature shows itself. And it speaks. One day I will be buried. Under the ground. And bugs will eat my brain and they will get a share of me. And her. And they will feast on parts that house your memory. And they will know. They will know what it's like to have lost her. They will smell it through the breakage of my body. And through the cracks in my skull. And they will know what it was like to be me. They will know. I grab a cigarette from my jeans. The smoke fails to rest itself in the air as the wind blows it away. The wind plays around with its victims. Psychedelic views build upon the visions of the sight in front of me. This would seldom happen. *God's creation*. I hope she's happy. But everything stays the same without her. I don't feel capable of driving. But I can't stay stranded on the side of the road either. I throw the cigarette on the floor. I stamp on it. That extinguishes it. I check the GPS on my phone, flipping it open. I'm met with an empty battery screen. It flickers on and off. Of course. There isn't much I can do. I will have to sleep in the car. Sleeping in that cramped space will be a challenge, but there isn't any other choice. The morning starts to come in, red turns into golden sunlight as it breaks through. It hits the muddied ground in front of me. It's cold. I can't afford to keep the car on for longer than thirty minutes. I open the boot and grab two bottles and one duffel. I sit on the back seat, unzipping and removing multiple pieces of clothing from the bag, covering myself to ensure I can stay warm. And I start drinking. And drinking. In an alcoholic haze my eyes finally close.

I wake up, dehydrated to the brink. I remove the clothes that were lying on top of me and I manage to wobble out. My legs feel numb. They're barely able to support me. I stretch out. I allow my body to wake up out of its heavy slumber. I take a few steps around to wake myself up before I start driving again. I feel the wind rustle through my hair as I speed up, letting my foot rest on the pedal. I still do not feel well rested. My eyes are still wine-red and my face has lost all of its colour, resulting in a horrible complexion. I can hear her speak.

———

"C'mon Leah, stop drinking. You've had enough."

I stood up, attempting to take the bottle away from her. But she didn't listen, nor did she show any care.

"Stop it Noah. Just let me be for once, okay? It's fine, loosen up a bit, you bought this for a reason, didn't you?" she whined.

I remember her attitude clearly. Her alcoholic ways were the same as mine. She would drink the day away until we were wasted enough to love each other. Our conversations were never rich in content; most of the time we would find ourselves hating every fibre of each other's being. We would command our hearts with disillusionment, acting as if everything was alright between us. It never really was in the first place.

"Leah. Stop it. Give it to me," I said, reaching out.

"I told you already to let me be, just let me be, please, I need this," she said. She took another sip.

"Leah! Give me the fucking bottle already!" I shouted.

"Don't yell at me Noah. I swear to God. Don't yell at me."

"It's the only way to get through to you. Think for

once. It might do you some good, you know, thinking for once. It isn't difficult. Well, maybe for you it is."

It was annoyance digging in between my ribs. She was a product of what I had created. How could I expect her to stop, when I was living it day to day. And I was there, always tugging at her to come back to reality when I wasn't even in it myself. She was a better person than me. It was written in stone. I knew that well. I knew it through looking at her proclivity to care for me. I knew it when I first laid eyes on her. But I couldn't stand it, knowing I was lesser. I was prey to myself. I leaned into unhinged efforts to stop Leah. It was stupid of me to even compare myself to her.

"You remind me of someone. You sound just like him. Your papa," Leah said.

"Fuck you, you don't mean that."

"But I do Noah, you have made yourself his spitting image."

"You're fucking drunk."

I stood up, pacing back and forth in the unlit room. Sweat on my skin. I could feel it stick against my clothes. I felt sick at the thought of Papa, and the fact that Leah brought it up made my chest hurt.

"Noah, I'm just joking around. It's okay, there isn't any need to—"

"Get the fuck out, Leah. You've said enough—"

I raised my tone, and got closer to her. My body language was hostile as my mind got clouded. I snatched the bottle out of her hands and threw it across the room. It loudly shattered against the wall. Trails of glass and alcohol were left behind.

"What the fuck is wrong with you! I didn't mean anything—"

"Get the fuck out! I want you out of my sight."

"What do you mean you want me out of your—"

"Are you stupid? Are you not listening to what I'm saying to you? Do you need hearing aids or some shit? You just compared me to Papa, huh? Really? Do you have any fucking idea what you said?"

"Noah. Listen to me, baby. Sorry, I—"

"Leah, you're a miserable person, you know. You're not even yourself without me. You are a load on me. You hold me down. But here you are still. Acting all pissed off when you know you need me."

"I do not need—"

"You need me to stay alive, do you realise that? You're nothing without me and you won't ever be. Are you that dense to not fully realise that yet? I saved you from that bottomless pit you were so desperate to get out of. Do you not remember that?"

"Don't bring up my previous life. You know how bad I struggled."

"Why don't we bring your father into the conversation too, then? Let's talk about the things he did to you, and bring it up in an argument. That would be a good idea wouldn't it, bringing up trauma to get reminded of, over and over and over again? Wouldn't you like that?"

"Don't you dare continue, Noah," she quietly said.

I was hurting her bad. But she'd hurt me too. She caused endless pain.

"I bet your mother didn't care too much when he touched you, did she? That bitch didn't lose any sleep over it. She might as well have fantasised about it like he did."

Leah looked at me. Fear on her face. Her eyes screamed vulnerability as tears began to stream down her cheeks. Her body started to shake.

"Why— why are you bringing that up now. Are you done?"

"Do you want me to be done?"

"You will no longer taint me, Noah. Look at what you've done. Look at what you've done to me. You made me think you cared about me. You do nothing with yourself. Nothing. Yet you still stand there. You still take the moral high ground when you're even more fucked up than I am."

"Shut up."

"Do you even fucking hear yourself?" she said.

"I loved you so much more than you loved me. But you bled me dry out of it. You have made a corpse out of me through the days I have wasted by your side. I wish I never met you, Leah. I wish you weren't so deceiving with your false promises, and your excuses all the damn time. Everything doesn't revolve around you. Not any more."

Silence filled the space around us. As Leah looked at me, I looked away. I couldn't stand to see her like this.

"And still it baffles me how worthless you sound... you've never done anything for me. You never will, will you? You don't deserve me, Noah. You break me until there's nothing left to break. You pretend you're picking up the pieces, but you really just collect them to use against me, you fucking asshole. Cause that's what you are, nothing but a fucking asshole. Fuck you. I hate you. I hope that hurts you. I hope it hurts like you've hurt me. I hope it digs holes in you. I hope you'll regret this. You definitely will regret this."

"And what about you, huh?" I said, talking through her.

"I've had enough of your shit."

My face was blood red. I grabbed Leah, and shouted directly into her face, spit flying everywhere.

"You think I wanted all this shit? I wanted a normal

life too. I wanted somebody I could trust my life with. But I got you instead."

"You're lucky you even got me. Where else would you be Noah? I let you be someone. I let you be whatever the fuck you wanted to be. This is what you chose. You did this to yourself, and you should take responsibility for it for once."

"You're a fucked-up joke. Who even wants somebody like you? You're a disease. You poison everything you touch. Every ounce of my being despises you. You knew who I was when we met. I could not have made it clearer. You know that. And you still decided to fall in love with me, knowing all of the shit I was dealing with. You knew that from the very start. But here you are, weaker than even submitting to the thing you were supposed to help me with."

"I was always there for you. I've been helping you since—"

"I thought you would. I thought you would try and help me but you never did. You never even tried to. That's what I will never be able to understand. Why did you never try to make us whole? We could have been something. I'll never forgive you for that."

"Noah, I—"

"Maybe if you tried you could've saved us."

"Noah. I have been trying. I've been trying so hard. Please."

I could tell she was hurting. Her sudden retreat from the ongoing altercation was deafening. It was shown through the stinging discomfort of the words she spoke.

"Leah, you better get out of my face before I do something i'll regret."

"Okay, don't hurt me. Please baby," she said.

"I hate you, Leah. You make me feel like the worst fucking person. I hope you know that. And for what?

You blame everyone but yourself. You did this but you're too stuck up to know that. Fucking narcissist."

"Please, calm down a second, let's—"

"And you make me want to die. Is that what you want to hear? You make me want to die. You make me want to have lived a life without you. I've become sad because of you."

"Noah..."

"Now I understand your father."

Leah slapped me across the face. In return I pushed her against the wall and wrapped my hands around her neck.

"I will kill you, you fucking bitch!" I growled.

As I could feel her disappearing, I loosened my grip. I remember I fell to the ground, crying at her feet as she moved her hands through my hair. The destruction is stamped into my skull.

It was the first time I attempted to end my life. Shitty mental health. Only a few days after this exact period. The resentment was so great, it struck me with a wooden stake. It broke my nerves. The idea of the sanctity of life had gone out of my mind. I felt like I needed to sacrifice the problem at hand to end our constant battles. I was no longer stuck in my head. I became a spectator to it all. I saw the grinding of my teeth chip away at my essential layers. It exposed the pain I had felt through it all. A priceless way out for suffering to end. I let my knife slice away at already existing wounds. I wanted to let my body bleed to death. I would find myself even more lifeless than before. My limbs were shaking at the thought of it. As my eyes watered up I saw the ill-fated reflection of myself in the splintered mirror. I held the knife up against my neck, slowly puncturing a small cut. A stream of blood trickled down my neck. Onto my naked chest. A warm feeling of euphoria came over me. I was playing with life itself. For a moment I held more than I could handle. I felt the cycle break itself through a regretful afterlife. It would guide me to where I belonged. The best revenge would have been to end it myself. I remember holding back, just out of sheer love. I could taste the idea of her finding me dead. It wasn't worth debating her suffering over it. Being compared to the thing I swore to ravage made reasons turn into more reasons. I saw myself crash and burn. The love did the same. The love had always been doing the same. I didn't want this any more.

I had never been more aware as the reflection smiled at me.

Quite a lot of time has passed. Leah would always ask to go out into the wilderness. She wanted to explore herself and who she was. I was always scared to give in to it. And now here I am. I can't pretend that there isn't any hatred within me, but I'm trying to detach myself from the person I hate to be. My intentions are pure. The life I have lived has not resembled that enough. *There is a being war waged.* Between the evil and good is where I find myself. And it still really hurts. I find myself dealing with so much shit that my chin starts to quiver. I feel my throat thicken at the possible answers. I know what has to be done. I have to stop with the alcohol again. To become sober. The idea repulses me. How can I expect myself to follow through with this, if it took me fucking years to run away from the apartment. It isn't viable. I exclude the thought. At least for now.

Mountains slowly come into view, appearing from

under the horizon. Clouds hang above them. Fields grow upwards. I have already travelled longer than the total span of a day. Different parts of my body are starting to hurt. Tingling sensations cover the whole surface of my legs. I should probably get them checked out. I get off the main road. Into a parking lot. There's a liquor store. It doesn't seem open. It wouldn't hurt to try anyway. I park in one of the empty spots. I get out. It's already nearly evening and there's a faint sudden change in temperature. I take my jacket from the back seat and pull it over my cigarette-stained sweater. I start making my way to the building as hoards of police sirens vaguely disappear into the distance. I flinch at the sound. I reach the entrance doors and realise they're bolted shut. A chain and lock holds them. I check the hours displayed on the door. I look through the window. It's been cleared out. I see it has been abandoned. As I walk back to the car I notice that I can stay here for a while. Maybe to get a bit of a grip. It will be a safer area than most around here. I drink. It relieves me. I roll down the window. I throw the empty glass bottles out. I still have enough to drink for a while. But my cigarettes are running low. I will have to suffer through it for now. As the pain in my legs increases, so does the headache.

I should just hit the road again. The police sirens appear closer. I see one of them pull into the parking lot. I feel panic rise. The vehicle comes to a halt, its siren on. I quickly get behind the wheel. I place both hands on it. *I can't let them fucking find me.* Sporadic thoughts whirl around in my head. I see the officer step out, and he makes his way towards my window. I roll it down and I'm greeted with a slight smirk. He looks dumb. And I look shitfaced.

"Good evening," I say.

He shines his flashlight into my face. Then around the inside of the car.

"Evening, sir. License and registration."

I pretend to look around for it. There is no possible way I will be able to leave here if I hand out this information. I don't want to be locked up.

"Respectfully, why do you need all of this? Doesn't seem like I'm doing anything."

"Routine check. We need to ensure all vehicles are properly registered and compliant with the law. You're also in an empty parking lot."

I glance around. The surrounding buildings stand in a massive U shape. I don't know my surroundings. I've never been here. I can't recognise anything. There's only one narrow road leading in and out of here.

"Do I have to give it?"

"It would be in your best interest. There isn't any need to escalate this."

I get lost in thought. I glance at my hands. I can feel my bones inside of them. Sweat runs along my fingers. It leaves traces on the wheel. I get nervous.

"What happens if I don't?" I ask

"You'll be arrested for failure to comply."

"Fuck man. Why do you make me do this," I whisper.

"What was that?"

"I can't give it."

"Step out of the vehicle for me," he demands.

"I can't do that."

I see his hand moving towards the gun at his side. He frowns at me and takes a step back.

"Step out of the vehicle," he repeats, menacingly.

An infrared beam dots my chest. My surroundings are lit up by blue and red colours. Everything is moving slowly. I open the door.

"Alright. Let me get out."

He takes me to his car. And I give him my identification. He runs it through the database. It takes a while to load. But it eventually does. My face appears on the screen. His eyes widen. He looks at me with fear. I don't give him time to process it. I run back to my car. I slam the door. I step on the gas. I hear the siren trail behind me as I speed out. I get onto the highway. Adrenaline fills my body and all of the pain I was feeling subsides somewhat. The night sky is grey and lit up by the street lamps. The road is empty. The vehicle rams into the back of mine. I feel the pressure of the hit push me forward. Fucking dirtbag. The window is still rolled down. I poke my head out letting the wind catch my breath. I breath in and out. Everything is moving slow. With one hand steering I aimlessly drift from lane to lane.

"Fuck. Fuck. Fuck." I say to myself.

Suicide by police. Sounds like a viable option. But is it really how I want to go out? No. I won't let this be the end. I reach for the pistol under the seat. I grab a clip from the centre console and slide it in until it clicks. I put it on my lap. I have no eyes on the road and my vision is blurry. Heat rises up within me. But I let the gun rest. I don't even attempt to do anything with it. I release my anger on the wheel by hitting it repeatedly. And violently. Nothing good will come out of this. Nothing good will come out of this shit. The vehicle behind me is still in sight no matter where I look. He is trailing behind me. I want nothing but to be able to end it all. To execute him. Or to trade lives. I feel psychotic and out of my mind. What the fuck am I going to do. Why did I put myself in this position. *God forgive me.*

'Man up,' I think to myself.

I swerve from one lane to the other as I check for any possible exits. And I catch sight of one. I'm driving faster than I've ever done. At the last second I steer to the right. I take a road off of the highway. The *kchulim* isn't able to stop in time. He misses the exit. I hear his tires screech on the asphalt, but by the time the vehicle turns around I'm already long gone. I keep driving for another five minutes. Stones and rocks hit the sides. In a panic I stop the car on an inclined street. I try to catch my breathe. I find trouble in doing so.

"Stupid fuck!" I cry out.

I start hitting myself on the head. Hard. Through the tears I grab a bottle from the backseat. I down half of it. In less than a minute. I lean back, with my hands on the back of my head. More charges added to my record.

Sunrise bleaches my environment.

There isn't much around here. Scenic views of the landscape cover most of the way forwards. The same goes for the way backwards. Maybe in another life could she have seen this with me. Power plants can be seen in the distant. A grainy glow emits from its tops. Transmission towers stand alongside them, and a train track encircles it all. The heat of the sun hits my windshield. It makes its way onto my hands. The warmth feels dry. Another town comes into view. As I drive through it's spiteful to me. Its appearance is very different from the last one I visited. It feels more familiar. As if I've been here before, which isn't possible. I look out of the window. I see a figure walking at the side of the road, from the street lights, giving the effect of a zoetrope. A sign signals me into the correct direction. I decide to find some refuge at long last. I think I deserve it. And I need it.

I open the door. There's a piercing stab that shoots into my stomach. I let out a soft grunt. But it doesn't bother me that much. It will pass eventually. I limp through the cobblestone-tiled town. Its yellow-stoned houses are covered with thick ivy. Fallen leaves cover its empty streets. Everything is closed, from the shops to bars. There is no life present at all. The omnipresent threat of happening lures me forwards. I get to a shallow lake. It runs under a bridge, and disappears out of view. It's lightly raining. It leaves ripples in the opaque water below. There is a scent of ocean water. It flows through my nostrils. It hinders my current state. *Memories of the east.* Shores covered in sands. Dark blue waters. Building sand castles. The way Papa would hold me up high. On his shoulders. Covering my body with sunscreen. Watching the waves break and letting out screams alongside it. More beautiful than land. Finding seashells. Pointing at seagulls soaring through skies. Getting lost in the waves of heat. And exhausting myself. Back when things were okay. I shake the thoughts away. A bench has been placed nearby. It overlooks the river in front. I notice another person heading towards it to sit down, and as my footsteps are heard reverberating against the surfaces, the figure turns around. I cannot make out its appearance due to the low light. The lack of features confuse me. They pat the bench, eager for me to come and sit down. Without any clarity I decide to go ahead. I sit down. We instantly lock eyes.

―――

5:27 a.m. The time when he died. I wasn't at his side. But Mama was. She caressed his face while he was lying there. She gave him kisses too.

"*You don't know him the way I did.*"

I did. I knew him very well. He got his voice

recorded. He put it on a cassette. I couldn't play it until a few days later.

"Noah. Since this is the last time you will hear me, let me tell you what I should have told you years ago. Your heart has always been full of regret. Break yourself open and let it go. You are not capable of changing the narrative. Forgive your past mistakes. You are in the present now. It's willing to forgive you. Do not yield to the same errors I made. I bore the consequences of my actions. Did you forget that I once tried to change them?"

He starts coughing.

"I will die with regret. There is no man to blame but myself. I know that. I wish I didn't lose words every time she came close to me. I wish I could tell her how dear she is to me. And when I was done with what she was, I found out how much I was in love with her."

How dare his words even leave his fucking mouth. Even now I can smell his stench. He had time. Plenty of time. He could have given Mama enough. Hand to God he should be thankful only the sickness got to him. I keep listening.

"But it was too late by then and my heart wept. I prayed no more and I started to get ready for my death. I tortured her Noah. Day by day. I never stopped. I hid compassion within the deepness of my heart as the alcohol tore me apart. She still took me back. And I still modestly took advantage of your poor mama. I took her dignity. Poor woman. She deserved a better husband. I found myself on the brink of self-forgiveness, every single time. I have become my sickness. I don't wish you to think of me otherwise, okay? Do you get me? Do not give in to the violent world. Don't get injured by what the alcohol brings. I held her. I held a human being. I crushed her. I turned her upside down. I let time devas-

tate her. I disfigured her. Even in our darkest days she would call me up, to ask what I wanted to eat, or what time I was going to be home. She gave me nothing but care. Not once did she inflict anything evil unto me. She never showed any less than she always did. She was an angel. She was sent from above and I will forever despise God for that. It is buried within me. An eternal cry. Maybe I will be reincarnated to be able to choose her as she chose me."

I found it difficult to listen. His voice would continuously break. I could tell he was suffering.

"Whatever you think of me, life has been deemed unfit for me. I chose to drink over taking responsibility for anything. I chose it over you. I chose it over Mama. I will now choose to take it to the grave with me. But do not reminisce about me. I am not worthy of it. I am a sad man. Nothing more. But I wish I could have seen you again. My son. My boy. Do not find yourself dwelling on what could have been. You have done enough. And a damn better job than I could have ever done. You go ahead and find yourself a decent way to deal with it. Empty yourself out. Pour out what you have to give. Express the pain you endure. I asked about you. To Mama. Even if I was never there, I know things about you. I can tell you are lost, but there is no shame in that. You are a man, and it is what you are cursed with. Find yourself once more. Make your mama proud, my son."

Can anything worthy of you be found in me?

Tensions filled my surroundings. It felt like I was in the same room as him. We are both confronted with revelations of ourselves, from birth to death. All I wanted was to have another conversation with him. A symbolic representation of our inner struggles engage in discourse. I understand the constant sorrow that plagues us. An invitation to the consciousness that so haunts me, and to a spillage of my future endeavours. I reveal myself. I find myself standing within the remnants of my former self. I see parts of my past through the breath I exhale. It is inescapable. Papa and I are more alike than I'd care to admit. Whenever I feel pure anger, I know I am still his son. It follows me with a hearse. It eats away the remaining desire to see Papa again. It doesn't help to get a reminder of what I should do from a person that had all the chances in the world to do what was right. To not act like a fucking tool. To treat the people that cared for him with an ounce of goodwill. He wasn't respectable. That would never change about him.

Let your wings be carved out of your very own flesh and bone.

I'm sitting on the bench. I find myself looking out into nothingness. The water sways from right to left, from one corner to the other and I am fixated on it. I don't want to look away. The balance is now more fragile than it has ever been. I become indecisive whether to continue my travels north. The alcohol has run out, my fatigue started coming back. I see everything through a different lens. I no longer feel. My body is weak. The drinking is slowly but surely making me perish.

"What have I fucking done," I say to myself.

It feels like the trip is a constant loop of the vision of my mind. I keep seeing the same road come into view. There is no apparent end to it.

Around an hour later I finally reach a motel. I definitely don't have the money to crash for long. It would be a shame to spend it on something I don't need to spend it on. Maybe the stop will prolong everything even more than it has to be. But I have to remind myself that I am not doing this just for myself. I am also doing this for her. In her memory I have to keep going, far away from the wistful feelings I let roam about. In every tree, in every mountain, in every road and in every possible fracture I see her. She is frowning down upon me. I no longer frown back. I see the world for what it is now. I see it for what it could've been. It couldn't have been much. People are dangerous. She did right by ending it herself. If not, *someone else might have done it for her*. I no longer hate what she did. It was never in my place. She freed herself from the hardship she was harshly subjected to. I look up into my rearview mirror. I see the hills fade into the far distance. I finally forgive her.

Chapter 4
Heavy Kisser

It's a run-down motel. It's obvious at first sight. The red neon sign hangs with one screw attached. A hazard for anybody walking underneath it. It seems unfrequented as if it died with the recent crisis. Its bricked frame is ruptured, creating an uneven textured surface. But it will do for me. The moon is a pendant in the sky. The white celestial body shines through my silhouette. I walk towards the entrance, taking a closer look at the inside. I can barely see anything through the smudged window of the front-door. I decide to take a leap of faith. The soft chime announces the arrival of my presence. The interior is a little better. The carpet softens under my shoes at every step I take. The blood-red walls show the effort put into it. There is nobody else inside. A small discoloured sign hangs on the corner. It tells me where the reception is. A glass chandelier hangs in the middle of the entrance. Its crystals reflect the subdued light emitting from the plastic flames inside of its holders. I start to like the place. I focus on its intricate details. I hope it's affordable. I walk over to the reception desk and drop the single bag I was holding at the sight of a woman. A siren. Her long, curly hair is tied up in a messy bun that matches the colour of her hazel eyes. My attention is riveted on her as she gazes at me. She has long lashes. Thick eyebrows. Her nose has a curved bridge. It's slightly smaller than mine. Her skin is light and clear. My ear is nearly pierced exactly how hers is, but she carries small gold hoops. And a small ring in her right nostril. Her lips are full. I find myself lost in her looks. Through her feral stare I can tell she is innocent. *Ruthless. Vastly unhinged. Catastrophic.* From the base of her neck to the arch of her spine. She's not where she is. *I'll take care of her.*

"No smoking inside any of the rooms. That is including here, there, and in the lounge area," she says, pointing towards different spots.

I notice the cigarette tucked behind my ear. I forgot about it. I don't remove it. I find myself stuck in place. I start fidgeting with my ring finger. I feel sure that I shouldn't let myself be taken by her. But she is damn beautiful. I see the reflection of my own future through the eyes of false angels. I drop the idea by the thought of Leah. Nothing compares to her, not even in an imperceptible way. I can't desire. I own a past to remind me that I am an infestation. An affliction of suffering. I have to keep my head on straight. My behaviour probably starts to become obvious to her.

"What can I do for you. Do you want a single?"

"Yes, that would be great," I reply.

I don't even bother to ask for a price. She doesn't even bother to smile.

"We charge by the night. How many?"

"Three."

"I need an ID."

"I don't have one on me."

"Any sort of identification?" she questions.

"No."

"I don't think I'll be able to give the room out without identification."

I pretend to search my pockets and my wallet.

"Can't you just make an exception this once. Please?" I ask.

A long pause follows. She looks me up and down.

"Alright, what do I even care. Don't make me regret it."

She steps from behind the desk. She signals for me to follow her. Her face appears stale. Neither of us acknowledges the awkward silence between us. *She is inviting me to an execution.* I watch her body move. I can't stop staring. Dread follows me as we make our way through the labyrinth of hallways, passing old doors with silver numbers displayed on them. I can hear people talking in the rooms. Bad build quality. We finally get to the room assigned to me. As the receptionist opens it I feel a surge of coldness escape.

"Sorry about that. There's a small hole under the window. Tomorrow it will be fixed. Hopefully," she says, half-smiling.

"Oh, it's fine."

"Here are your keys. Bathroom is shared and it's located at the end of the hallway. If you need anything, I'll be at my desk. Enjoy your stay."

I softly grin at her as she leaves me be.

The room reeks of wet laundry. Paint is half rasped off of its beige walls. There is a small window directly in front of the door, high up. To the right there is a single bed. It's barely big enough to fit a person my size in it. I am above average height. There is a desk, parallel to the bed, with a wonky chair under it. I notice marks on the wooden floor where someone has dragged it. I put my bag down and open one of the drawers. It is filled to the top with coffee-stained papers. Probably something that the previous guest left behind. I pick a few up. They cut at my skin. Needle-sharp edges. I scan the words; legal papers, something about money issues over a property. I note the address in question is the same as the hotel. Probably something I shouldn't get involved with. The room hasn't been properly cleaned. I didn't need anything more, other than a few nights to sleep. The ceiling isn't high up. With a bit of a longer reach I can touch it with my hand. The room is dusty. It's much bigger than I expected it to be. I sit on the bed. I let myself fall on the mattress. My head hits the pillow and I sigh audibly. Nothing is happening around me. I appreciate the peace. *The gates. Inward and outward.* No bathroom in the room, I notice. I pick up the keys. I exit my room, making sure that it stays locked behind me. At the end of the hall I find the bathroom. It isn't in pristine condition either. Mould grows on the sides of the walls, and around the bathtub, spreading itself along the corners to the sink. I've seen worse places. The idea of developing a sickness doesn't bother me. I rush back to my room. I undress. My body is a cemetery of scars, bruises and burns, each one telling a story of its own. Punishment, humiliation, regret. They render stunning colours on the skin. I remember how she traced her finger along them. I lie back down on the bed. The alcohol I drank is still dulling pain in my chest. But everything is getting thicker and more swollen by the day. I can feel the coldness creep in from the open hole. It won't disturb my sleep. I find myself listening to the wind outside hitting the window. I close my eyes.

The hills speak your name.

I'm woken by an unspeakably loud banging from the room next door. The banging is followed by argument. And yelling. Two voices. I grow uncomfortable by the second as the argument grows louder in volume. Is nobody going to check on them? Did God prepare me for this very moment? Am I supposed to step in? Or should I let it slide, and mind my own business. I stand up, not feeling very well. I start putting on my jeans and shirt from yesterday. I sigh loudly as I open the door. More guests are looking out from the safety of their rooms. I can see the alarmed looks on their faces. The receptionist is already there. She's knocking, trying to get an answer. The door doesn't budge. The screaming becomes ear-piercing. I walk over to where she is standing, and at the exact same moment the door opens. A girl not older than around twenty runs out. Dry blood covers her clothes. She looks around with horror, but she doesn't say anything.

"What happened? Are you okay?" the receptionist asks.

There is no response from the girl, and she starts making her way to the exit. The receptionist runs after her. I glance at the man inside of the room. He is older, maybe around thirty-two years old, and as he tries to stand up I step inside. The room is similar to mine, but at a quick glance I make out some key differences. The window has newspapers taped to it. It keeps out the light. And any unwanted eyes. A warm blanket of foul smell hits me and I scrunch my face out of disgust. There is barely any air to inhale. I have to step out again to hold myself together. One of the onlookers confronts me.

"This isn't the first time. We've had issues with this room before. Always the same guest," she says.

I enter the room again, ignoring the warnings from the others. The man looks vile. He's lying on the bed grunting, and as he sees me approach him he stands up, mumbling something under his breath. He looks at me, and smirks. Degeneracy flourishes from his face. There is unsurpassable violence swelling up within me. There's tightness in my chest. Red mist overtakes me as the man laughs unpleasantly. I walk over to him. I throw him back and I unleash the anger I have held back for so long. I hammer his body, throwing my weight into my fists. Built-up fury releases my ill temper. I can't help myself, can't stop. There is pain streaming through my hands, and as I look at them I see cracks in between cuts. Blood starts to pour out from between my fingers. The more I hit him the more pain I feel. I'm digging up the mistakes I desperately needed to get away from. But I still don't stop. He falls to the ground. I keep hitting his face. He starts spitting out some blood. I catch my breath at the sight of it, and I finally pull away. The man crawls to the wall. He lifts himself up, and puts his back against it. I look down at my knuckles and notice the skin slowly peeling off. The flesh underneath is exposed.

"You should be thankful you're still breathing," I manage to stutter.

The police show up six minutes later. I feel sick at the sight of them. Hopefully they don't recognise me. They arrest the man. They take me aside. They don't arrest me. They know the girl. She lives on the street, barely getting by with the work she does. She get's treated like she's disposable. They told me this wouldn't be the last time this would happen. The receptionist appears, and asks if everything is okay. Something seems concerningly off.

"Yes, everything's good. Are you okay?"

"I'm okay, yes. Did you see that guy's face?" she questions as she rubs her arm.

"Yeah. He deserved it."

"Oh for sure he did. I'm Yasmin, what's your name?"

She stretches out her arm, opening her hand up. She likes the fact I beat him up.

"Noah. Do you smoke, Yasmin?"

"Yes I do."

"Want to go out for a smoke?"

"Sure, Noah," she responds.

We walk towards the bathroom. We go out the back door, leaving a trail of whispering voices behind us.

"So, where are you from?" Yasmin asks.

"Just a couple hours away from here."

"Are you happy?"

"Am I happy? That's personal," I laugh.

"Just asking Noah, with everything that's happened since Leah."

"How do you know... how do you know about Leah?"

"I can see your past through the way you look at me. Through your eyes. I knew that since the moment you walked in."

Yasmin looks straight into my eyes. I can feel myself being reckoned a failure. She slowly leans in. She holds me. With pressure. Her hands are soft.

"What would your mother have thought?"

———

I'll let it take me. It doesn't feel like home any more. The sun keeps shining the same. There is no warmth left for me. I've prayed for the shore. I've prayed for some good grace. I've prayed for restlessness. I've prayed to be able to love her again as I used to. It shouldn't be this hard.

It shouldn't be this fucking hard. September. September. I will fuck you up. I will fuck you up so bad. Deformed. Rip out my hair. Slice my face. Break my nose. Make it more crooked. Burn my insides away. It beats me to my knees. And I take the hits. I'll let it consume me. I'll let it. I'll mix water with vodka. Wine boxes. Clear spirits. I'll hide it. I'll let it consume me. I'll let it. It's a curse to exist. I've murdered myself.

I wake up on the floor, drenched in a mix of sweat and alcohol. An empty bottle lies on top of me. A terrible pain strikes my head. I hear the banging continue. I bring my fists up. I notice there isn't a single scratch on them. The screaming and yelling has stopped. In its place there is discourse going on in the hallway. I start to inhale and exhale in a distraught manner. I don't know what has just happened.

"What the fuck is going on with me," I say to myself.

I promptly get to my feet, and put on the same clothes as I did before. My surroundings start to spin once again. I find myself losing track of how many times this has occurred. It's hard to keep my balance as I walk towards the door. The wooden floor beneath me seems to shift into a thin tightrope. The pain gradually increases with each step. I reach for the doorknob but I am unable to. There's a force vigorously roping me back in, dragging me back to where I lay. *Sink me into the floors.* The walls illuminate me for who I am. My shadow alters its twisted shape into a horrid being. It consumes the space around me. My tired eyes fail. *My tired eyes fail.* The inability to act on my well-being is swallowed whole by the abyss. I collapse and I start to gasp for air. I plead for the restless hours I spent contemplating life itself, and the sleepless nights until morning breaks. At least then I knew what I was. Who I was. I had somebody to hold on to. Had a reason to continue. To swallow my violent pride for the sake of another person. I have broken out of a cocoon at the wrong time. I've wasted the everlasting thoughts of death that infest my mind. The whole room is shaking, and there are people banging loudly, questioning what is going on behind the closed door. I scream and yell. I pound the walls. I envision Leah scurrying out of the room. She's running away from me. *The end has a grasp on her.* I stand before myself as a slave to grief and regret. A silhouette masquerades across the room in the shape of me. It extends its reach. Its blurred outline acts as the truth of what I present myself to be. I bask in its expected presence. I feel its stiff hands gripping on my neck, suffocating me as hefty pain washes it away. I hear droplets fall on the floorboards. My hands are dripping with blood. I notice the empty bottle has been shattered. Glass pierces my flesh. I try to extract some pieces, but I can't. I curse at myself. I lower my body position so I am now sitting on the floor, tucked against the bed corner and the door. I quickly sweep the rest of the bottle under the rug. I hope it won't attract any unneeded attention. Without notice the door opens. The receptionist is standing in the doorway. Her facial expression says enough, and as she opens her mouth to speak nothing of importance comes out. I stand up, holding my right hand in my left hand. The pain is intense.

"Don't worry about me. I dropped a bottle on my hand. That's all," I hesitantly say.

She keeps looking at me in shock, and doesn't react to what I said.

"Shit. Can I help?" she says, getting closer to inspect my hand.

"That doesn't look good. Come with me."

I don't say anything. I keep my mouth shut. She takes me to the back of the motel, to a small claustrophobic office space. She pulls out a metal box. It has some medical supplies. I hold my wrist tightly. I create thick red lines around it. I don't converse with her. I let her use tweezers to remove the stuck glass. I groan at every pull, but there isn't really much pain anymore. I feel nauseous even while sitting down. I find it difficult to concentrate on anything other than the surgical process at hand. And I finally sense some judgement. She doesn't sugarcoat my existence, and sees me for who I really am.

"Sorry if this hurts."

"Thank you for helping me, Yasmin," I reply.

How do I know her name? She never told me it. I notice the name tag neatly pinned onto her white shirt. It reads 'Yasmin'.

"Is that better, Uh— what's your name?"

"You can call me Noah"

"Please be careful, Noah. I'm willing to keep it to ourselves this time, but I'll have to kick you out if this happens again. I can smell it on your breath."

"Understood," I say.

"Okay. I bandaged your hand. Again, be careful please. If you need me you know where I am, okay?"

I say thank you and walk out of the room towards my room, with the feelings left behind me. I close the door, resting my head on it from the inside. As minutes turn into hours, the realisation of Leah not being there deepens. My heart beats in the rhythm of what used to be hers. It demands to be set free. It's found in the hushed disappointment of myself. I grapple with the turmoil brewing within me. I am still in love with someone no longer alive. How can I see myself moving on from that? My heart still aches for her, like it did the day she passed.

Everything was found in the suffering.

Days pass. Loneliness keeps getting worse. I start to feel comfortable where I'm at. Violent sandstorms have started raging outside. Travel doesn't seem viable, not until they've abated. At least not for a little while. I barely talk to anyone, and I find myself bumming around the place, searching for literally anything to do. Yasmin comes to see me every day. I try to keep my distance. I couldn't provide the attention she wants. I make it clear, always finding an excuse to abandon the conversation. I've found out a couple things about Yasmin: She's a student at the university. This is her summer job. She isn't in a relationship (not that it is any of my concern in the first place). She likes painting, and she has shown me some of her art. We have a lot in common. She also reads. And smokes. She's done anything from weed to opium. I don't want her. Don't want to want her. I want to keep it that way. I have never doubted my commitment to Leah, even after death. I see common connections being made to Yasmin. She reminds me a bit of Leah, only through some sort of a distorted aspect. *She's wearing her flesh.* I promised Yasmin I would help take some pictures for her yearly student ID. I might not do it. I feel myself getting too close to her. I am not open to moving on. I don't have any plans to do so. My greatest addiction is Leah. Even sobriety wouldn't save me from that. Maybe forgetting will, but my past is fused within who I am. It would mean losing more than I have ever lost. I can't fucking afford that. I don't think I will ever get past her. But I don't mind. To have a love clench your throat at every step brings some clarity. It brings hope that I might be able to change. It stops war between my desires. I know what I need. I need her to guide me. I've always needed her. But for how long can I adhere to what I say? Isn't there going to be a point of no return, where I must accept the change I want to profess? I'm already repaying my wrong-doings. Until how far can I push the narrative that Leah is the angel on my shoulder. I feel betrayal even considering her to be. I should be the devil on hers. Am I keeping her trapped within my consciousness? When do I need to give her rest? All of these questions fill my mind as I look into the nothingness of the landscape. There is more than meets the eye. I take my phone out to revisit the SMS messages I left. The messages aren't spaced out. Heavy texting from my side. Responses from Leah fill the screen, substance lacking. I ask her where she's been. The texts refer to the bridge, and the desperate begging that follows hints at what happened. I told her how much I needed her. I begged her to come home. I praised her. I again begged for her to come home. Nothing worked. They read as a memorial. It desensitised me to almost everything else. A person could never prepare themselves to see such gruesomeness on display in front of them. Leah lay lifeless as I held her in my arms. That was the last time I saw her, until the white sheet was laid to cover her. She did it so quickly. She didn't give any time to explain herself. I don't know how I dealt with surviving the following days. I remember barely holding on to what I had left. I also remember I didn't in the end. I turn back to what I was doing before my vulnerability opened up. But I don't remember shit. I realise my memory is getting blurred. I notice the vodka clutched in my left hand. I drink myself into oblivion.

There is no schedule left for the passing of time. Only the past catches up to me.

Leave me be. Please, leave me be.

More days pass. Yasmin frequents my room more often. She doesn't really know how bad I get, but that's okay. Lost in thought I get interrupted with a knock on my room door. I stand up. I open up. Yasmin stands in the corridor. She asks if I'm down to help her take some pictures. I follow her to an uninhabited room. Theres nothing but a table in the corner of it. She hands me a camera. She poses against the wall. Yasmin keeps making eye contact. I feel my heart skip beats. I try to keep myself collected. She makes me hard. She keeps looking at me. Her lips broaden to the sides. I can tell she likes me. Her face doesn't give away too much. But I can tell. It shows with her body language. It shows with her wholehearted care shown towards me. It's practically plastered on her face. And I don't even pay to stay here any more. She stopped charging me for the room. It lifts worry off of my shoulders. I take some more pictures. The flash always goes off too late. I show them to Yasmin. She appreciates my help as she looks through them. She heats me up. She's nicotine. She's the alcohol I pour down. But I don't desire more than a friendship. That is what I keep telling myself. And that is what I will keep telling myself.

———

For home use only. It flies by like a jet does. You don't know what to do any more. Out in the desert and your hair blows in the wind. I let you touch me but you scorch me to ashes. Why are you doing this to me? Human-

sized grief in between the smallest instances of you. Don't sell me kindness any more. Sell me what I deserve to buy. Don't try to heal me. I've done it all to myself. I'll let you slip away, just in case you would like that. Would you? Your eyelashes spread your wishes. And I look into your pupils. But under the burden there is nothing to wish for. You have all you want. Unless you want me to let you slip away. Just in case. Some of us will be okay. You're a weapon. A tender, soft-hearted swelling in my lungs. I will keep it so it develops. I'm growing feathers for you, so I can fly away like a jet. And I will be able to let you go. Just in case you want me to. Subtle signs are shown at your centre. I've been there. I'm stuck in its maze. I'll find some wings, and attach them to my skin and bone. Like Papa told me. I have no desire to keep you waiting for me to leave. I know you find it hard. That's why I will do it for you. The morning after. Or in a week. Or in a month. Or in a year. Or never. I'll stay as long as you keep forgiving me. I am your spine. None of those others know you. I am part of your anatomy. Claw me out of there if you want. I'll let you go. Just in case you want me to. She's playing with my hair. And the couch is warm. You don't know what to do any more.

Most of the time I find her sitting outside on the front side of the motel. She looks out into the open space. Nothing is happening. But nothing ever does around here. I've always felt isolated. I've borne my isolation with me. For some it's a circumstance. For me it's innate. And there she still is, so I go and sit next to her. To escape from my head. We don't say anything for a bit, until she talks.

"Are you in a relationship of any sort?"

The question catches me off guard. I feel it. I smile.

"It's a bit complicated Yasmin," I reply with.

"Sure it is," she says.

A long pause. I don't know her story, and neither does she know mine. There is nothing to judge. There is no story yet.

"Are you?"

"No, I'm not. I recently got out of one though. A really bad one," she quietly responds. She tilts her head to the side as she breaks our eye contact.

"Oh man. Do you mind me asking what happened?"

"Not at all. He was very abusive. Hit me whenever things didn't please him," she says, lifting up her shirt. Multiple purple bruises are revealed.

I feel compassion towards her. Nobody deserves to be physically hurt. Especially not Yasmin. Her sweet attitude outshines everyone else's. She's had violence inflicted upon her. My mind wanders, thinking about how I hurt Leah. I never once punched her, or had the thought to do so, but I was close to it on occasion. I used to threaten her, impulsively. I always regretted it.

"That's fucked. I'm glad you got out of there."

"Yeah, well. I don't have a good relationship with my parents either, so I'm kinda just doing this all on my own, you get me? What about you though?"

"I can relate. My ex— she passed a while ago. My mama did too, it's all very heavy shit. But I get through it."

I try to repress the release of unwanted emotion. It has been a while since I talked about it with anyone. The last time was with Elias. It didn't end well.

"Noah. I'm very sorry. And here's me thinking I have a bad past," she says.

"We shouldn't have to compare. We're the lucky ones,

we're still breathing. Everyone has their own shit to deal with."

We both stay quiet. We absorb each other.

"Anyways, It's getting late. I'm heading back, talk to you later?"

"Of course Noah."

I head back inside. I know she cares for me, but to what extent would this go. She doesn't even know who I am or what I've done. I will never be able to tell her. She would reject that version of me. In all certainty she would even reject this version of me. But why even bother asking myself this? I don't have any feelings towards her. The more I tell myself that exact thing the less it becomes fucking true. I peek at the window. I see that there's no light outside anymore. It's evening. I am in need of a drink. I head back outside. The sky is purple and pink. The lights down below are the only surviving source. Yasmin is no longer there. I walk towards the reception, and there she is. I ask where the closest bar is. She points me in the direction.

Night beacon.

It's cold tonight. The area is desolate. The road is relatively close to the motel. There are bushes lining the side of the building, imitating the colour of its outside. I walk further along the grass paths. Fireflies sway in the air around me. I reach the bar. Exhausted. I'm looking for some cheap liquor. I let myself in and sit at one of the stools facing the counter. It is fairly busy, with loud chatter overtaking the ambience. I signal to the bartender. I ask for a drink. And I drink. I don't stop. Glass after glass. Cheap alcohol. I am brutally in need of it.

Leah would take me to sell with her. Sometimes. She was damaged. It was hard on her. This specific day was really hard. We didn't have any money. We couldn't survive without it. His beard was unshaven. His clothes did not look in the best state either. His facial features were masculine, but there were traces of tolerance and sensitivity to be found in his voice. His complexion was pale. Rough irritated skin. But I minded my own business. She took me. It made her feel safe. We were at his house. The lights were on. He liked talking. And fucking. He saw Leah looking at a picture of his son.

"He was around your age when he died. I miss him a lot. He couldn't hold the weight of loss anymore. He felt like it was his fault. Like everything was his fault. I still see him enter the house every once in a while, bit of an unwelcome guest but that's really just what it is."

"I see," Leah said.

"I don't mind his presence every now and then but I can't seem to move on with myself. I'm muted. I've been drained of any happiness he left behind. It's a constant ache that overtakes everything around me. And all I hear is this bullshit talk about silver linings, and meditating, and learning how to cope when all of this will never bring him back to me again."

"Mhm."

"I hope you don't mind me talking."

"No, it's okay. But it'll be taken off your time."

"That's okay. His girlfriend called it in, thought she was taking the piss at one point. She found him bled out on the bathroom floor. What a sight that must have been for her. I couldn't— I couldn't believe what I was hearing. Bled out in— what? Bled out in the bathroom? It

didn't tie in with reality at all, but when I saw the scene my eyes nearly popped out of their sockets! So much gore, and blood. He slit his whole throat open. There was more life in that gaping hole than I'd ever seen. He didn't have anybody else, only himself so when you lose sense of that too it's hell brought on you. He should've listened to me, that sweet boy. Do you have any kids of your own?"

"No. I don't," she said. She quickly looked up and down at me. There were unspoken conversations in her voice.

"I hope you don't. I'll never forgive him for it, nor will his girlfriend. I always think he owed her an apology of some sort, for the problems he inflicted on her. He paid the price in full for some fucked-up reason. Don't know what I've ever done to deserve it, but I'm sure he had his reasons. I didn't sleep for days after that, I thought I turned into an insomniac. Started taking all of these different pills, contacted centres, all of the generic shit you should never do. His girlfriend broke up with him shortly before, but I can't really blame her now can I. She thinks it's all her damn fault, that selfish bitch. She still calls me up to make sure I know how bad she feels, but not damn once has she asked how I feel. I wish I could tell her that he really didn't love her that much at all, and saw her more as somebody to get drunk with. Couldn't even attempt to save him, wasn't there neither was I. That's where you are lucky, you only have two people to deal with. I got three of 'em, not to mention I don't even care for two. Could find me hung in the back bathroom if I got the fucking chance."

We don't say anything. We just look at each other.

"Don't worry, I won't do that. I don't like pretending that I don't know what I'm speaking about. I know you know I've attempted. I know I've battled my days, and weighed my options against each other."

He was a regular. She'd seen him before. They'd talked already.

"Leah says you always think about her. It's a beautiful thing, really. A struggle to cope with irreparable loss now defines your very aliveness. Isn't that romantic. Don't wait too long, Noah, for you are nothing more than a candle waiting to be put out of its burning misery. You know it's true. It's been a while now, and you've forgiven her for it, haven't you. Forgive yourself too for God's sake. It's not her fault. I mean, just take a look at her body. Who wouldn't want to touch her all over. The world's filled with enough assholes as it is. I'm one of them. But we don't need 'em now do we?"

My fist clenched shut. I had to leave. I had to wait outside. She said he wasn't gentle. I wanted to kill him. She had to hold me back. Wildflower. I nearly killed a guy. Yet she did it for us.

A few minutes pass, and the truth becomes apparent. I came here to better myself, but I'm still wallowing in the eternal pleasure of pity. No attempts have been made to change that. It wasn't going to happen by chance. I'll have to live through it. I stumble out of the bar. Laughter is left behind. I find myself standing in soft rain. It hits my face with warmth. I bawl at the top of my lungs. With hope comes a new day, and with a new day comes more remorse. I try to get myself together. I spot Yasmin standing at the doorway. I walk towards her, and she notices how drenched I am.

"Noah. Come inside! What the fuck are you doing out here?" she shouts.

I don't respond. I go to stand next to her. I don't say a word as she waits for something to happen. It doesn't.

Silence stays in its place as my heart stops. Awkward tension fills our surroundings. I look her in the eyes. But I don't feel anything. Anything at all. She doesn't know who I am. She will never know who I am. I head inside. I know she feels something for me, but I can't say the same back. There isn't an inch of my body that lets myself be free. My eye twitches at the thought of Yasmin's affection. I arrive back in my room. Nausea overtakes me once again. My body cramps and aches through its suffering. My breathing becomes slower and more difficult by the second.

Devotion always turns violent.

I lay down on top of the unclean bed sheets. I pick up my notebook to read about past days. A constant reminder is necessary. It binds me to the essential persona of who I am. I don't want to lose track again. I flick back to the day of Mama's passing. I reminisce through the words written in cursive. The sentences grow to be filled with more despair each time I return to them:

Thursday

I said goodbye to Mama today. As I write I know she is no longer around. I am completely losing it. The pain feels immense. I will write everything down in hopes it will help me get through it. Very unlikely, but I might as well try. She knew it was time, I think. I didn't though. I hardly know anything anymore. She didn't give in for months, even with her passing being an eventual fact. It must have bothered her. Or maybe it didn't at all. She didn't even recognise me. I cried at her side, holding her hand and crying at her confusion. It was fucked. She kept whispering but I couldn't make out the words as much as I would have liked to be able to. You told me something about taking care of myself. About seeing life having a certain end instead of being an obstacle to overcome, and you might be right but what is there to live for at this point? I just can't find myself to be grateful. I fucking hate it here. Is there even anything to chase? Is there anything at all of importance to me? Do you want to live within my mind? Do you prefer to be let go? I'm in need of help Mama. There was no decency given to you whatsoever. It didn't even let you leave as the person I fucking knew. You left as a stranger. I didn't get to say goodbye to you. Maybe I'll say it eventually. I don't think I will. Rest easy. Love you.

Friday

Shit hasn't gotten better, not even in the slightest. I've practically alienated myself from everything that was left. I don't know why, but fuck. I guess it'll have to do. It's nearly been a week now. They came asking for you Mama. Went to empty out your place. I couldn't bear to tell them what happened though, you know how I get, so I lied. I know that's not what you want to hear, but they don't deserve to know. They weren't there for you, even when they knew about the cancer spreading. You mean more than a funeral, or words spoken from the mouths of these people. You deserve to be praised, at the least. I don't really know where I'm getting to with all this. I find it worthwhile. I'll keep repeating that until I start to believe it.

Monday

Got fired today. Apparently I was too much of a cost. Got into a fight with the guy too. I'm ashamed but what can I do about it? I find it really difficult to be around myself lately. And I feel like I'm the only one that actually has to deal with all of this shit. I don't have anybody. I'm lonely. I miss you.

Sunday

It's getting bad. Things around me are shifting out of shape. I can't make out where I'm going. It feels like I'm in a constant trance. A constant high. I find it difficult to stay awake, but there's the same difficulty in sleeping. I can't get to it. And there it is again. Someone keeps playing the piano upstairs. It's beautifully eerie, but it gets interrupted by cries in between the notes. I can't make out if it's a woman or a man, but there seems to be a lot of misfortune brewing there. They pierce through. They keep me up late into the night. But I don't find it annoying, I feel for them. Everyone has problems here, it seems. It isn't a place you would like to have seen, Mama. You wouldn't have been comfortable with me living here. But it's okay, it's home. I don't want you to be disappointed in me. I am trying. Anyways, it is really none of my business what my neighbour does. I don't think I should intervene even if I hear a blade-saw go off. At least I get to enjoy the fucking piano every now and then. It sounds sad, but it fills the time. Besides, that's the least of my worries. Hopefully they have cigarettes up there for when I visit.

Friday

I walked through the forest today. As a matter of fact, I'm in that exact place right now. Heavy with grievances I haven't gotten over yet. I'm sorry. I like to imagine you're still around. I tried to find you in the noise of the leaves and I tried chasing it, but you ran off. Another time I'll try again. I'm living in fear Mama. I'm drinking too much and my consciousness isn't the same as what it used to be. It's unclean, and I feel disgusted by myself. I know the remedy lies within but I can't seem to get to it quick enough. If you were here we probably both wouldn't be able to recognise each other any more. But I can't stop. Not for now.

Monday

I met a girl, Mama. It's real, it's so pure, and she fills me with a type of ecstasy I can't really explain in words. I haven't spoken with her yet though. She might not like me. But I saw her from a distance. I'm happy nonetheless. I also met the guy from upstairs. He seems nice enough to get to know. I don't know what to do, but honestly, I'm looking forward to the future for once. I don't have anything else to write. That's it for today.

No Date

Sorry that I haven't been writing. I've fallen for her. She found a way to cut off my wings. I've found myself a step further from you Mama. Maybe I'll come with her instead. Maybe. I'm trying to be a man of my word now, because Papa wasn't and I don't want to become like him. I promised you that. Remember? I won't break promises any longer. I'll try my best not to. She's making me feel love Mama. She's showing me what you've always wished I would see with my own eyes. Here it is! We saw each other again today. Something's changed. I think it's the way I look at everything now. Life might be worth living, but it'll have to be with her for sure. Otherwise I don't want it.

No Date

I'm not sure what I've done. Will God punish me? For what I've done? Mama I regret it so much. I wish you were here. It's eating me alive. There was blood, so much blood. I don't deserve it. I don't fucking deserve it any longer, please let me fucking end it, I can't stand it anymore. What have I fucking done. I am worse than Papa now. You will never forgive me. Leah will never forgive me for this. I broke my promise. I really did this time, and there's no way out of this one. I hope I rot. I hope I fucking rot and never see day again. I hope my corpse gets ripped to shreds and my blood leaks like rivers do. Bleed me dry, angels. Drill holes in my eyes. Piss on my fucking carcass. Cut me apart, hack my limbs off.

Sunday

I wish I could've had one last conversation with you.

I never get to re-read this far. The memory of the last passage overwhelms me, but I can't exactly place my finger on what caused me to write with so much emotion. There are no dates for two of the written pages either. Much of my memory is clouded. It's unrecognisable even to myself. I'm not surprised by the absence of it. I don't linger on it too much.

The less I know, the easier it is.

Chapter 5
A Stone's Throw Away

It's been a couple of weeks at the Motel. Yasmin and I have grown attached to each other. I don't know why I've ended up desiring her. I want her. I want her pulse. It somehow feeds me well. We spend the days on the front porch, reading and talking about whatever comes to our minds. Rays hit our faces. I find her laugh so contagious. The way the dimples on her face appear. How she puts her arms behind her back every time she looks at me. The days grow longer. The sun takes longer to rest itself. I feel happier than I've ever been previously. Yasmin knows the perfect chords of me. Our shadows cast onto the cement in coordination. I allow myself to enjoy the little days I have left. I've kept my alcohol addiction to myself. I've had to. The secrecy of it undermines how much effort it took to get here. For now it's necessary.

Tie a plastic bag around your head. You should gape for air.

———

Yasmin is staying at the motel herself. She asked if I wanted to go to her apartment in the city for a couple days. I was hesitant to answer. I knew the police would be searching for me, but I couldn't deny her request. I have been travelling alone for a while. It would be good if I had some company with me. I have to leave soon anyways. This could bring me further up to where I want to go. I wasn't going to waste this chance. I still think about Leah often. My growing fondness for Yasmin affects my thoughts. I no longer feel like I'm betraying Leah, but rather accepting that she will never come back. I've tried to leave it behind. There isn't any other way to cope. I still miss her, but I also have to think about myself in order to prosper. I can't do that if I stay stuck on something no longer viable in the first place. Yasmin grabs my hand. She pulls me out of my thoughts.

"Is everything okay?" she gently asks, noticing I was not completely present.

"Yes. All good, just a bit tired."

"Yeah, it's getting kinda late. Do you have any?" she says, signalling with her hands that she wants a cigarette.

She looks at me with a sarcastic smile.

"I think I do. Yes. Here."

"By the way, I got shit news this morning," she mumbles, as she places the cigarette in her mouth.

I do the same, and reach over to help her get it lighted.

"Which is?"

"Granny passed. Old age. In her sleep," she responds, nervously fidgeting with her fingers.

"Oh fuck. Are you okay?"

"Yeah, I guess so. I didn't know her that well. Only

met her once," she says, exhaling all the smoke in my face.

"Fuck. Sorry to hear. I'll pray for her. Are you sure you're okay?"

"Yeah, don't worry. Do we have the car ready for tomorrow? We can't leave too late," she says, clearly showing her pain.

"Uh huh," I answer.

I can tell she is holding back heavy tears. She tries to hide it from me. I let her.

The day passes quickly. Before we know it the sun is setting. I find myself contemplating many things. I don't want to stop watering my addictions. I've never done that for anyone. And I never will. She won't understand. It isn't how it's supposed to be. And the world keeps laughing. I open my notebook. I start writing down whatever comes to my mind:

I promise you no longer have to worry about me as much as you used to. You cared. That is all that matters. I promise that you are the person that still makes me feel safe, even through the turbulence of what remains. I no longer feel like I have to hold it in any more. I promise that I love you deeply. I know I never made it clear, but my heart has always accepted it. I hope you are proud of me up there. I hope you look down with a hefty smile. There is nothing more for you to give. You have given me more than I am worth. What a beautiful story you have made out of me. I promise I will keep existing. Can you believe I am scared to die? It would mean losing you completely, and at least I carry you with me now. There is no overarching plot any more. You took it with you. But I promise there is hope and love and support out there for me, waiting for me to reach for it. I will try to make sure I laugh again. But I will wait for our wounds to heal, and the pain to stop. Let your guard down, and rest, for me, and for us. You deserve it.

The morning comes fast. So fast that there was barely any time to think. It's still very early, but I decide to get ready for the drive ahead. Everything is packed. I won't come back here. Whatever happens next won't change that. I see Yasmin standing outside already. I carry my bag outside and she spots me. She runs to hug me.

"Thank you for coming with me. I know things aren't easy for you either," she says, with her face pressed tightly against my chest.

We walk towards the car. I load the boot up. She has way more baggage than I do. As we pull away I look behind. I give a silent goodbye to the place. I already miss it. It gave me some sort of belonging. At least while I was there. The sign still hangs loosely. The path is as sandy as ever. The bar stands as crooked as I last saw it. The bushes wave in the wind. We speed away. New thoughts conspire. The city shouldn't be too far away. GPS only says a couple hours. And it only takes a couple of short hours.

"I've always been watching the door. I couldn't help myself. I waited for it like I deserved it," she said.

The orange light hit the hill we were sitting on. The white oak provided some cover. Her mascara was running down her face.

"That's the trouble with it. It turns you fucking rabid."

Her bruises were slowly fading. But they are there. They are there.

"I hunted it down, when he was the hunter and the wild beast. He gutted me. I saw so much in him I kept waiting for it to get better."

I was holding on to her words. But she doesn't understand me. Almost every time I see her step on the edge of losing control.

"And he wanted everything from me. My sexuality. My feelings. My fantasies. My mind. My appetite for him. And he kept taking more and more and more until he started to react with physical abuse. He couldn't help it. I know he loves me still. I also do. He didn't do any of it on purpose. I hope he gives me another chance."

Yasmin's body language changes. She dreams about him. She still doesn't see him for who he is.

It is now evening. We arrive on the outskirts. Brutalist architecture fills most of the space around us. Concrete rows of monolithic buildings rise directly from the ground. It exudes a bad vibe. Rough textures, and angular lines intersect each other with precision. They cast shadows across the avenues. Community doesn't emerge from the rigours of this urban area. Resilience is not nearly as enduring as the structures from where it originates. It isn't hard to notice that there isn't much around. After twenty minutes we arrive in the centre. The city doesn't sleep. The buildings are covered with twisted spires that pierce through the thin air above. Mist covers the road ahead. Traffic glows through with its coloured auras. The noise however doesn't offend me.

It hits lightly on my eardrums. The streets are not busy tonight. A historical tram passes by through narrow stone arches, intersecting the road we are on. It brings with it a tremendous rattle, shaking the ground as it passes out of view. We cross the bridge, with its medieval architecture boasting its history. Its statues and implications are jailed in its grey stone. With the calmness of the water still beneath us, there is a sense of fragility. Silent apartments fill the cobblestone streets and the streetlights generate a certain softness. Only in memory does the city sleep, with its past blanketed by the atmosphere that surrounds it. My body grows weary. I grab my notebook from my duffel. I scribble down everything that comes to me. I use rolling paper as a bookmark. The tear and wear of the pages serve as the memory of the written work. I write:

I have always felt a disinterest in the city. Its monopoly posed a threat to my ideals. The busyness of it all was never in my interest in the first place. But this is different. It speaks of two worlds at once. It connects the dots for a comfortable existence. There is a lot of beauty to be discovered here. Hopefully I will let myself discover it. Maybe it will be a distraction from life fucking me from behind. Maybe it will make me suffer. Nothing is certain. Nothing is certain in a city like this.

Around thirty minutes pass. We arrive at an apartment. Yasmin tells me precisely where to leave the car. I see her trying to contain her excitement.

"I haven't been back here for a long while. It feels really strange to be here," she quietly says.

"Thank you for letting me come with you Yasmin."

"Don't thank me. Keep that bullshit to yourself," she laughingly responds.

"But I mean it. For real."

"You can thank me later," she whispers, leaning in.

Nestled within a quiet area of the city, the exterior of the building stands half intact. The wrought iron balconies hang above our heads. Its cascading vines fall in front of the curved windows below. We head through the weathered entrance. We walk up the stairs. We only have three large bags. We reach the third floor. Apartment 3B. As I step through the wooden doorway, I smell the aroma of a foreign fragrance. Above me, a small circular window filters in moonlight. It casts patterns across the floors. There is only one room in the apartment. A narrow staircase leads up towards the bed. A lantern hangs in the middle of it. The muted palette is accentuated with the accents of the art living on all the walls. A Mosul rug hangs on the wall. How can I allow myself to be blessed with being here when I'm not deserving of it. I won't stay long. I sit on the bed. I tightly hold my chest. The pain has still not disappeared. Only God will have a say in it. Yasmin sees my reaction to my discomfort. She tells me to sit on the bed. She sits next to me.

"Is everything okay?"

Every subtle move she makes puts me at peace. Her soft feminine endeavour to reduce my pain makes everything sufferable. She catches me looking at her and smiles. I smile back. Tension builds in the room. I can't help but notice her. She instils angelic fervour in me, something that I haven't dealt with in a long time. In the midst of it, I feel like I'm beneath the surface. Hesitance casts doubt on my affection towards her. I find myself entangled in a silent dialogue of desire. *The bridge burns out of fear of vulnerability.* Something binds us tightly together. Through the incertitude. She lightly touches my hand with hers. She commits. She interlaces her fingers with mine. Yasmin looks at me with tender eyes. I can tell she is painfully holding her breath.

"What are you doing?" I quietly say.

She nervously kisses me. There is drug-like addiction on her soft lips. It feeds my mind with the fragility of who I am. It's laced with ecstasy sweeter than honey. She holds my arms tightly together. I kiss her back. Our eyes are shut, and there is conflict circling around me. I see everything more clearly than I ever have before. I run my fingers along her face. Only heaven could feel this good. Now I can say otherwise. It's a kiss that wildness conspires in. A kiss that soothes the sword's release from my chest. It resurrects the chaotic bloom of my body. It reminds me of the beginning of February. I want to surrender to it, but I don't know how to. She could be the right person, but the time never seems to be right. And that's the simple truth. Something draws me back to the temporary pleasure. I let myself go. We fuck.

We could have been more than traitors. We should drink to that.

I find myself lying in bed with Yasmin that night. Her arm is wrapped around my body. Her skin feels soft. She is mumbling in her sleep. Whatever I do, I cannot fall asleep. I realise what I've done. My heart is beating out of my chest. Betrayal rushes through my veins and seizes me with all its hold. I feel unfaithful. I know what I've done. I've started the process of replacement. My lips start to quiver. I rub my eyes with my hand. I can feel the alcohol demanding control over me. It betrays a newfound self. Addiction always comes first. I slowly get out of the bed. My feet try to find the steps in the darkness. I hope she won't be woken up. I walk towards the bathroom. I turn on the water. I wet my face. I silently stare at myself. Fucking ugly. I tilt my head. Everything turns. I don't want to be here anymore. I want my Leah. *I want her. I want her.* I want her so bad, please God. This has raised me. It's no longer acceptable. For the first time, I am more than afraid. More than silent. More than raw. *The mirror is dirty.* I rummage around. I try to find anything to drink. Cupboard doors opened. Items misplaced as I scout the bathroom. There isn't anything. I'll have to go out for it. Fuck it. A nearby shop should sell some. I grab a used plastic bottle. It has her lipstick on it. I get dressed. I throw on anything I pull out of my bag. Stained jeans. Grey shirt. I quietly head out. The keys hang in the door lock. It's never easy. It never is. The time is 12:10 p.m. Most places are closed by now. But it's worth a try. I step outside. The disillusionment starts weaving its way in. There is no other possible outcome. I will have to show Yasmin who I really am. I can't help it. I have to warn her against myself.

Self-destructive dickhead.

I walk until my blisters bleed. I find myself at a small corner store, which is open. I pause for a moment. I stand outside, allowing myself to smoke the last cigarette I have left. It brings a special calmness. A comforting shroud that hugs my lungs. I stand there. The ash covers my fingers. The windows in front flicker with faint signs of life. The distant hum of traffic provides a backdrop to the silence. I put out my cigarette. The embers sink into the air. I enter the shop, and I ask for the alcohol section. The bright lights hurt my eyes. The bottles are once again lined up neatly, each with its bane. I don't take my time to choose what I want. I grab the cheapest one on the shelf. I don't have a lot of money. Back outside I open it up. I empty a few drops into my plastic bottle. I am desperate. Desperate for something to take over. Desperate for something to drag me away. I fear myself. It demands itself to be felt as if inherited through a generational curse. I have been fed with boundless ideas. Emotions keep running feral. Is this what I always wanted? Or am I slowly leading myself into nihilism? The bell tower chimes. It awakens me on the spot. My aspirations are gone. What is left is the wanting. It doesn't bear down delight as I once hoped it would. I no longer want to be part of my existence. If only the past would stop catching up to me, I could let go of it. Then I could be unbound. I keep walking.

I reach a wide bridge crossing the river down below. Some narrow steps to the side lead downwards. There isn't anybody around. I start to walk down. The clatter of my shoes on the stone steps echoes. The river reflects yellow light onto the bridge. Ripples appear on the surface. I walk further along the side of the river, and, as the bridge disappears from above me, three sandstone buildings come into view in the distance. Broken window panes line the second floor. The rest don't even have any windows. One part of the apartment block is covered in debris. It looks like it's been hit by a missile. It reminds me of the fragility of home, and how much I miss it. The home Mama comes from. I've wanted my whole life to have given more to her. She made a home out of nothing. She turned the broken ground into marble floors and decorated my heart when I couldn't manage to do it myself. She must be badly disappointed. She must be. Seeing what I have done with myself, with this life she provided me.

The same words makes my breath catch in my throat. I start to slowly sway back and forth. It hits me hard. What a beautiful life I have led. Being blessed with the people who have enriched everything around me has saved me a lifetime of misery. I can only be forever grateful for it all. They have made the unlovable lovable and minimised the pain. I know I can never repay them, not because they are no longer around, but because I cannot bring anything of fucking worth. I have tried and tried but there is nothing left to try for when I cannot find even the slightest bit of worth to keep for myself. The mirroring in the water reflects only my worst features. It wants to drown me. And I feel so much. All at once. An overwhelming amount. The world around me feels shallow. The river calls my name. I take a few steps forward. I feel my bones crushed from the inside. The water stays calm. I am full of violence. I can't find myself to bring scarring to the undisturbed surface in front of me. I think a piece of me can no longer be found. I need to accept that. Every day Leah fades a bit. I started to forget the little things she would do. It hurts to know the days make you forget, and I try so hard to hold on to as much as I can handle to allow Leah to remain here. There is too much shit to deal with. Everything is an apparent crossroads. Everything is ill-defined.

Her body fell so quietly that I didn't even realise it happened. My memories have holes in them. Don't act surprised.

———

I sat with Elias. Early morning. Before the heatwave started. We talked about the first time I broke up with Leah. I put my trust in him. And I know I could. We weren't really friends. We never really were anything.

We were just two guys who knew each other and were dealing with the same shit, in the same place.

"*I also decided to move on. I had so many hidden wounds. They were refound in the form of cicatrices as my body started to heal. I reintroduced myself over and over again until there was nothing left of my former self, Noah.*"

I lit up a cigarette. And I took a sip from the bottle. He waited for a response. But I was only listening.

"*I found myself engulfed in a wave of grief the night she cheated. It seemed to expand with every passing moment. I used to be a sanctuary of her memories until it turned into nothing at all. And I felt guilty for allowing myself to continue living. I started overlapping. I started doing all of this different type of shit. I started longing to feel bad again, so she might feel sorry and we could connect again. Even if that meant I had to survive in some sort of constant heartbreak. I started to execrate my current life and partner and treating her the same way I did with my previous one. Even if she hadn't even done anything wrong. And I regressed. And I deteriorated, I made myself deteriorate, for something that would never fucking come back anyways, you get me, Noah?*"

I always found his voice calming. It had calmness to it.

"*I have nothing to offer her, man. There's nothing to me. It never really leaves you. It blemishes the world around you and makes sure it reminds and mimics and then reminds you again of the pain you have once felt. Sometimes things don't get better, they only get worse, you know?" I said.*

My leg was shaking. I could tell Elias personally cared about me. It helped. He said, "The more you attempt to cling on to nothingness, the more you start promising lies to her. It gets worse that way. In every aspect. I promise you that."

"What can I do man? She's all I have."

"Well, be present with her. Be honest. Be open. Before she starts distancing herself, because then it's over. Don't make her wait. I know about waiting. I've done it myself. I waited and waited for sand to travel upwards in an hourglass, can you fucking believe it? I fought and fought against the changing feelings but guess what Noah? It only left me worse off. I felt more betrayed by myself for waiting. It was a silent admission of defeat. But don't feel weak or stupid for admitting any of this. We are all human and for each and every one it is our first time living."

"Yeah."

"Nothing is or will be perfect straight out the box, not like you want it to be, because if that would exist, what would we even strive for? We need to make mistakes, Noah. We need to be able to make them to know if what you have is fucking real. But don't keep making the same ones."

"You're right," I reply.

"Healing doesn't come in remembrance. It comes in forgetting."

I try to listen to what everything inside me tells me, but I feel stuck to the idea of causing devastation. What if I decide to move on with love? I will remain the same person as I always have been, and the sacrifice of not allowing myself to love is the turning factor I should be devoted to. How can I expect hope to carry me forward when I only find hope in Leah? I drink more. And I can tell Elias doesn't want to see me drink. I gulp down as much as I can handle. I nearly drown in it. I can't keep my head above water.

An hour later I arrive. As I make my way upstairs I get ready for the inevitable argument. But it never happens. I enter the apartment and Yasmin is awake. She doesn't look angry, or disappointed. She looks worried. *Worried to the brink of fucking tears.* I'm sure she can smell the alcohol in my breath as I approach. She looks at me as if I killed someone. As if I tied them to a chair and waterboarded them. I'm no longer used to that. The look on her face says more than I had bargained for. It would've been better if she started screaming and yelling. I try not to let it get to me. We stay in silence. Her eyes do more than talk. They scream at me. They tell me to put the bottle down. To stop surrendering to my urges. But she doesn't say anything. She understands. She understands that I know all of this bullshit advice already. She knows I choose this even if it means the end. I stay seated on the sofa. Yasmin turns around and walks up towards the bed, and while doing so she turns off the light. She still hasn't said a word. It freezes my feet in place. How is it possible that I find myself nourishing off of Yasmin's kind deeds. She's allowing me to stay here with her. She's given me a roof. She's invited me in only for me to give myself up to my addiction. I don't head to bed. I stay up and sit on the sofa. I live in the silence. Her reaction caught me off guard. For the first time, I get the urge to do better. To be better. There is something within me reaching out to her, asking her silently to help me be what I need to be. And she does. But I don't allow it to happen. I don't allow it to have any repercussions. Yasmin is still a stranger. In every sense. I haven't let her in. Not properly. But I do not have to. If I do, I might lose that too. *Solitude. Solitude. Solitude.* I take my phone out. I head to my contacts. I leave a voicemail.

"Leah. I've been sober a handful of times, and I've had a few years under my belt now, and I've always let myself be led to the bad side of it, you know? And, uh, shit... I can't seem to get there without you. I don't even want to try. We had such a beautiful thing, and... fuck man. And, uh, I think I might be starting to run out of gas. I'm running out of gas. I've got nothing left to give. Not to myself. Not to anyone around me. Like, I can't hold up like I used to. I know you would fucking scream at me right now for not trying but that's what I needed Leah. For you to scream. And you still do in my head. It scares the hell of out me. But the drinking. It's just— it's just tearing me down slowly. I feel ashamed to call this number and sit here and cry. But I'm tired. It's wearing me out. I'm tired. I really am. I feel hopeless about getting back into the programme. I know that's what you would have wanted me to do again. But I can't. I think that's the main reason I'm calling you. Because I don't know how to get that belief back again. You only made me feel that. I don't think I could do it one more time. I don't know how to live sober. And I depend on myself to be able to. It's a lot of pressure. I'm not strong like you think, Leah. I didn't grow up like you. Fuck. And I don't know how to handle shit, man. I'm trying real hard, but it's getting harder and I'm starting to fuck things up and every day reminds me of you. And I've been thinking about what you said. About the gambler, and how the gambler just keeps fucking playing until they lose. And I'm just playing to lose. I think you're right. But I don't know how to stop it. I don't know what I'm trying to say to you, and I don't even know why I'm leaving this behind. You know, like, it seems like the right thing to do would be like, well, Noah, take your dumb ass to a fucking meeting, or just do something about it. And I hear that. But it's not that easy anymore. I can't just do that around here. I've been, over and over again. I drove two fucking hours away to go to one where they couldn't help me for shit. Over and over again I tell myself that I don't have to drag myself through it. But I do. I do anyway. But here's the deal. I need you. That's it. I need you and I need you and I need you and I will always fucking need you. I'm lost and desperate for a way out. And I want to feel good. Once. I want to enjoy the years, the seasons, the weeks, the days, and the time given to me. And I wanted you to have pride in me. I wanted you to feel like you belonged to me. But that's not the case. And it's killing me. It's the end of me. I don't know why I'm telling you all of this. You're not even there to listen."

It reminds me of the first day Leah and I met, and how she looked past all the problems and misfortune I found myself in.

―――

We found each other in a dead winter. The air was frigid. The trees had perished. It left behind nothing but uneventful days filling the calendar. Fortunately, I was out. Unfortunately, at the time, it was because the seclusion forced me to. I found people in the alcohol. It made more sense. It meant I could choose. It meant I could decide who I wanted to trust. Humans are no longer worthy of blessings, but the visions of the ones in my head were. I found Leah in a coffee shop. I stood outside the glass window. I was covered in grey snow when I saw her. She was just standing there. It was none of my business. I couldn't help but stare. I looked like some sort of creep. But she didn't see me. I decided to go inside, to keep myself warm. I hadn't had any social interaction in a while. The anxiety was building up inside of me. I was too afraid to mess it up. I didn't want to show her the things others had so easily run away from. My lips deflected the words I wanted to say. I didn't say anything at all. But I happened to feel our timelines intertwine. I sensed a far-fetched future spinning around in the air, riding on our exhaled breath as it mixed. *Out of harm's sight.* A pre-written existence so obvious I could have caught on to it even earlier than I did. It was almost obsessive. I noticed her imperfections within a few seconds. I loved them. Her eyes were slightly different colours. A part of her ear was slightly folded. But I didn't know her. I didn't know her and I had to back off. It felt miserable. I wanted to see what we could be.

And then I saw her again a few weeks later, in a bookshop I visited often. I had spent days craving to see her again. I wanted to rip out of my skin. I wanted to walk around town naked just to catch her attention. I thought maybe then I would be recognised. It was tormenting. I was in a relationship with a person who didn't even know of my existence. The fucking loneliness, of course. I already knew she carried things inside of her only I could fully understand. Then I finally managed to talk. I asked her out for dinner. I should've asked for her number first. She must have felt creeped out. But she agreed to it. It wasn't much. I know I didn't have that much to spend, but I wasn't going to let myself sabotage the situation. There was something about her I couldn't place my finger on. It felt more real than it should have been. I felt alive, in that moment, and after not having been alive for months, it was angelic to feel the rattling through my body. And I knew she liked me back. You could see it through her giggles and smiles, her stance, and how she stood there acknowledging me like I was someone deserving of love. I wish I had told her. I wish I pushed my sorrowful feelings to the side and told her how beautiful she looked.

She had a boyfriend at the time. She left him. She

stopped seeing him. I started seeing her more often. I showed her more than the house she came from had ever done. As time went by it became exhilarating. To know someone cared for you unconditionally was more than I had bargained for. My head couldn't wrap around it. I was a stranger around myself with her, and when everything died down after a day, I would fall back into the person I did not want to be. And that was devastating. To be so closely attached to a person. You lose yourself in them. It drains your lifeblood. Lines got blurred. I suddenly allowed myself to become faithfully one with her.

Then came the day she found out about my problems. She showed up early. I was wasted. There was vomit on my chest. The place was a mess. She took a break from me. And she left for a while, longer than I had anticipated. She made me feel bad about myself. She tortured me with her departure. I had not dealt with loneliness and the agony that comes with it in so long. The stranger that I found in myself once again appeared before me. It had me in a chokehold. It only made everything worse. But that wasn't her fault. Everything was mine. I never fully accepted that. I blamed everything and everyone else except for myself. I've always done that. I kept a huge part of my addiction covered under a blanket of lies. It was possibly the worst thing I could have done to her. It might have changed a lot in our end. For both of us. Destruction followed me when she wasn't around. It taught me inhumane things.

Pay for my mistakes and I'll pay for the coffee. Then leave before the sun goes down.

I'm still sitting on the couch. I look up at Yasmin. She's fully asleep. I can't feel Leah's presence. Maybe because I feel so unfaithful. I want her to come back, badly, and replace Yasmin like for like. These godforsaken thoughts eradicate all the hope I have left. Grief has become the person I am. I still fuck up, with even the best things given to me. It's like I don't care enough to move on, and I allow myself to stay stuck between the alcohol and what could have been. Born with the gift of feeling, so I can feel the curse of myself placed on me. I don't go back to bed; instead, I stay up the night, falling in and out of consciousness. My eyelids struggle to stay open. The bags under my eyes keep getting puffier with the days. I'm still not sleeping properly. Nothing has been working effectively. The pills I bought still sit at the bottom of my bag, and besides, they don't even work. Neither does anything fucking else.

I find myself still sitting on the couch, drowsing away, in a slouched position. The memory of yesterday is opaque. I slowly sit up and everything comes back to mind. Yasmin is awake already. She has placed a blanket over me. She's just sitting there, in the chair opposite of me, watching with a slight smile on her face.

"Good morning. How did you sleep?" she asks.

I can tell she's pretending. She knows my issues and wrong-doings. She is well aware of the problem I have. But she doesn't want to accept it. Yasmin has had a different image of me. It's now been corrupted. But she doesn't care. She just acts like nothing happened, which is nearly as bad as if she did act like something happened. I smile back.

"I slept fine. And you?" I ask.

"I slept well. I guess I was tired from yesterday."

"Yea. Me too," I hesitantly respond.

I still do not give in. I accept that she doesn't want to

remember yesterday. I let it play out. I constrain her thoughts. I don't allow them to develop into something she will despise me for. It feels selfish, but it is the only way I see out, to get away from the suffering. I still have to forgive myself for it all.

We don't talk for a while. The room grows colder with each passing minute. I can sense that there are words unspoken. But Yasmin never says anything. She gives herself up to it. And it hurts like a bitch. But I also do not say anything. I cannot risk losing more than I already have. The feelings for Yasmin stay the same. And she is miraculous, the way she still carries me forward even after seeing me in the state I was in. I know she didn't want to see me that way, but I don't care. As long as she pretends, I feel well and held in her arms for how long it will last, because I am damn sure it won't. I head to the window, breaking the immense pause. I open the window. I look down at the street below and the rooftops ahead. I light up a cigarette, and another one for her. We lean out. The morning takes our problems. It handles them with care. Muffled city sounds arrive from the distance. Birds fly past. There is some peace in the air, something that lightens the smoke. The palace is visible from here. I can barely make out the sharp point of its spire. Yasmin holds my arm. She scoots closer to me. We interlock our fingers. It feels nice. I struggle with understanding the feelings she has for me. I know it hasn't been long since we started seeing each other, but I wonder if she's thinking of something more serious. Her body language shows love, the way it flows in and out. And its shapes rest closely fit against mine. Wounds are still fresh. Some are starting to close, painfully creating visible rifts on my skin's surface.

Hopefully, Yasmin won't be the one to pry them open. *Don't leak me dry.*

The weeks that follow are spent in her embrace. She shows me a version of myself that I missed seeing. It shows up like a familiar face, but filled with uncertainty. It has an unknown presence connected to it. Terrifying at first; seeing someone so close as yourself unrecognisable in the view of another is another step closer to something worthwhile. And it's worth it. My addiction starts to lose its power over me. She's there through the burnouts, and the breakdowns and I feel like being sober is possible. But there are still many occurrences of me drinking. I can tell she has difficulty keeping up with it too. I don't want her to succumb to the pattern, like Leah did. But I can tell she is.

I had never seen Yasmin drink before, but as I unload my pain into the alcohol she starts doing the same. Hungover. Itching. She starts getting similarly drunk. Nearly as much as me. It's so out of character that it frightens me. She was such a gentle person. I eradicated that. Ever since that one night, I changed her. I formed a starting addiction inside of her. It's an incidental concurrence. But it's not all bad. The alcohol also makes her more appreciative of me. I don't mind her being drunk. When she vomits everything out, I clean her up. I take the chances. I want to feel whole again. Even with someone else. I start putting myself above everything else again, glorifying myself. I go to clubs. I go to parties, do the wildest drugs and have one-night stands with every girl I talk to. Every weekend. It keeps the addiction going. The euphoria holds me back from the good things. And I hurt Yasmin, just as bad as I did with

Leah. On purpose this time. I'm still learning the ins and outs and I'm doing a shit job at it. Yasmin doesn't mind. She always helps me, no matter what happened. Leah never tried. I always find myself asking why she never did. Is there even a reason to miss her any more? I'm not sure there is. But there are bigger things to worry about. My time in the city is ending. I have to leave soon. I'm getting worse. I've known for a while that I need to rid myself of Yasmin before I find myself creating another living corpse. It's not much of a decision. I want so badly to conform to myself and act as selfish as I have always done, but I can't do that to Yasmin. I think about the outcome this time. The first time I realised this was back at the motel when I saw her love for me start to shine through her portrait of herself. Its colours were so bright I knew it deserved more than I could ever give. Her touch was delicate. Perilous for me. From the first day I met her, I knew it could never last, even though it did last longer than I ever thought it would. I didn't know I had it within me. Especially not after Leah. Mornings kept arriving, and nights never disappeared. I could barely differentiate between them. They were all experienced in one continuous blur. I rarely have ever depicted my life to play out the way it has, but in the back of my head, I know there is untruth to it. I still experience everything through a shattered lens. Light still refracts through different shards to mislead my wrongdoings. Yasmin deserves more than I am, because of who she is. Her talents and attributes triumph over what I can ever be. *I seem to be able to take lives.* We're not officially dating, but we treat each other like we are.

I said I wished I could fall in love. Now what the hell is left of me but shattered bones?

I remember when I begged myself to leave her. I kept letting myself have another day, so I could spend it in her company. And the next day kept coming around so fast, every time. Through the agony I see visions of early Sunday mornings, sharing cutlery while warmth touches our tanning skin, humming stories that can be shared without words, or finding the younger me as an adult. As long as she sticks around. The breaking of a cycle. That is the beginning of everything. I wished today never came, but it did. The city is wearisome. And I'm in the same state as yesterday. I look next to me. Yasmin is still peacefully sleeping, covered with the blankets. I will miss her. But we cannot be saved. I can't allow this to go on any longer. For the first time, I understand why it must end. I don't struggle with that. I do struggle with the invoked feelings. Even through this all, I find Leah here. I haven't let go. I know I never will. She is one with me. We still find ourselves tied.

There is a distance now between me and Yasmin. I barely answer any of her attempts at conversation throughout the morning. They barely get through to me anyway. In the quiet corners of my existence, I find certainty cohere. Its web expands far beyond the sadness. I sit on the edge of the bed and I let my chin rest on my knee. I can see my ribcage poke out beneath the pale skin binding it. I touch it. I am witness to the never ending unravelling of my damned past. Her breathing has been counted before. Two out, and one in. I have already begun to rehearse the words, over and fucking over again, and the burden only grows heavier. The last hours loom over me. I have to leave the sanctuary I have burdened myself with, and its chaos in the form of this chamber. Unresolved conflict will always stay unresolved. I need to get rid of the expectation of an outcome found in peace. I don't even know how to bring this to Yasmin. I know I'll make her feel like shit. Suffocation drags me down. I'm seeking myself back. Through the cracks of desperation. My mind is focused solely on the day, and gathering the strength needed to follow up with fucking misery. My fractured spirit is clear in the newfound morning. The chained binding of us feels broken by will. Or at least it will be soon. But I know it can no longer keep going in the way it has been. To mend all of this would mean to sacrifice my body and myself. I take a deep breath. I steel myself against the rage. And as I open my mouth to utter words I will regret, she talks first.

"Good morning baby," she whispers, and reaches for my arm, planting a few kisses on it.

I feel my skin react, and my hairs seem to react to the feeling. My eyes search for hers. They meet. I feel okay.

"Good morning, how did you sleep?" I respond.

"I slept fine. Can you open the window, I'm fucking boiling," she says, covering her forehead with one hand.

I rise and open the window as she asked. A warm gust of air bursts inside the room. I sigh.

"What's wrong Noah? You seem stressed."

"We have to talk."

"Talk about what?" she says, frowning heavily.

I get up from the bed, and our gaze disconnects for a few seconds.

"We just have to talk, later. After you're done with the day."

"All right baby. Can you tell me what's going on?"

"Let's talk later," I say, slightly annoyed.

"Okay, but I want to talk about it now. You can't just expect me to walk around all day knowing you have something important to tell me."

"You'll be fine."

"You're taking the piss, Noah," she angrily says, placing her hand on her head.

"What did I do? I just want to keep it for later. It's not a big deal."

She looks at me. And her clenched jaw relaxes.

"Fine, you're right. Sorry. I didn't sleep well."

She rubs her face with her hands and heads to the bathroom. I follow her. I watch her get ready. The way she moves around always seems so flawless. She puts her hair up. She gets into the shower and I study every inch of her body. Sometimes it is difficult to look at her. The marks on her still match mine. It makes me feel guilty. Perhaps she knows of my intentions. Perhaps by chance, God grafted ideas into her subconscious. And fed her with the realisation. Or perhaps not. Who really knows? I watch her leave. She holds my face for a while. Then she kisses me, softly. I close the door behind her. I hear her footsteps travel down the stairs.

The silhouette of the palm trees. The warm wind. The call to prayer. The barechu beginning the morning blessings. Before the aliyah. I try to find it. I search for it. It feels like I've forgotten something. I wanted to wait at the horizon. I wanted her to tell me it would all be okay. I wanted to stop hurting her and to stop making her lose her worth. I wanted so much. And she did too. We were separate. The last moments of life. The last moments of us. Divided. Embattled. The alcohol brought us back to it. We thought it brought back us. That's why we got lost in it. But it never did bring us back. It never did. It made us not only lose us, but ourselves too. She didn't recognise me. I didn't recognise her. It was like being with someone new. But it wasn't new at all. The pain and sorrow and appreciation and recollection and pleasure was still around us. But we didn't recognise it in each other any more.

The day went on like normal. I couldn't help but question if I was making the correct choice. Blood will spill. It will again be found smeared on my very own hands. It feels much easier to just pull the trigger. To press a gun to my dome and let a bullet blast it wide open. To let myself be consumed with anything else but this tension tightening inside my veins. I kept telling myself that I needed to wait for fear to leave before I started to love again. But the fear is back. And I find myself in love again. I know what's coming. The feelings of dread are built up within me. I feel my choices leaving me flustered. I can't deal with it. How could I ever deal with someone of her calibre. Fuck it. I have to end it. I have to surrender to it. The day passes. Slowly. Yasmin has not arrived home yet. She isn't picking up her phone. Neither are my messages being replied to. And there is hunger waiting in the apartment. All of this pent-up dread is throbbing in my head, and thirsting to be released. She has to come back eventually. She has to. She wouldn't just leave. She wouldn't just leave me behind. She knows what I'm going through. No, she wouldn't do that. She couldn't. I have her by the throat. She needs me. I know she does.

It is now 10:46 p.m., and the evening has long consumed our building. Where did she go, did she decide for herself to not watch me leave? How does she know? How can she not. Were her feelings not as mutual as I always thought them to be? It doesn't matter anymore.

My efforts quickly become useless. My phone vibrates. I get a message from her. It's a voicemail.

"Hi, Noah. Uh, I don't know how I'm going to say this to you but I don't think this is going to work out anymore between us. You're a great guy and all it's not that but—"

She's talking through tears. I can hear people in the background. I don't know where she's at.

"I thought you would make me feel better but everything has never been worse. I'm losing it. I've never had any problems. You came and all of this shit just started in my head and I don't know how to get out of it anymore, Noah. I don't know how to get out of it. I've been holding on to so much ever since we first met. I can't talk with you. I've never felt like I could sit down and talk with you. You scare me. We're not made for each other Noah. We're not. It's a hard pill to swallow and I'm sorry, okay? I'm sorry I can't tell you this in person but I'm leaving this all behind and I have some people to help me with it and I need to take what I can. You've been everything to me but I've not been everything to you. It's okay. It's not your fault that you're like this."

I want to hold her.

"That comes out wrong but it's how I feel. I can't keep pushing it down. My ex has been there for me when you haven't been there at all. I wanted to be like you. While you went out and had fun, I wanted to go out and have fun too. You left me all alone that night, Noah. I got raped. You never noticed. You never fucking noticed. I called you so many times that night. I thought I was going to die. The only person that was there for me was Sender. Where the fuck do you think I slept that night Noah? I've seen him a couple times since then. I don't want to keep pretending to you that I'm in love with you. I mean, I was but I can't be anymore. You can understand, right? Please, Noah. You should understand. I'm not coming back to you any more, okay? I can't do it. It'll only make everything harder than it has to be. Stay as long as you like there. I'm not coming back home. I'll miss you but I can't be close to you anymore. I'm choosing for myself this time."

The screen goes black. I throw my phone across the room. She never came home. And suddenly, I was nothing to her. I'll always be a stone's throw away from the creek.

Stay to listen. Stay to listen. Don't leave. You shouldn't leave.

Chapter 6
Solar Retinopathy

Sadness slowly devours me wherever I stand. I felt a lot for Yasmin. She's gone out of sight. A sharp pain finds itself permanently dug into my chest. She made me this way. Maybe it was just the idea. The idea of having found something worthwhile, to distract myself from the undying love I have for Leah. Or maybe it wasn't. It doesn't matter now. Fate has settled it. This is what I've paved. What it could've been, or what it never could've been isn't important. I seek her between the foreign faces, but she is nowhere to be found. Yasmin never owed me anything. I guess she wasn't mine to love. She never really was. There's not much else to it. I do not cave in. I do not make it more difficult than it has to be. But I find calmness in the distance I have created for myself. The weather is warmer than the month before, and its heat burns my skin. The sun still shines through the window panes, and life carries on even heavier than it did before. But I carry it well. I think I do, at least. Her voice still carries me forward. It puts grace on who I have slowly become. It has now been weeks since she left, and as I left the city behind, much of who I once was stayed behind.

With her. She moved on from me. Decided she couldn't handle it anymore. Fair enough. Even I can't. But I miss her. *I fucking miss her so much.* From time to time. I feel like I fucked it up. I haven't had a drink ever since. It might not seem that long, but the itching says otherwise. Withdrawal symptoms have already started creeping their way into me. Sickness arises. It manifests physical and mental burdens. Delicacy turns into shards of glass. It cuts into me. My head pounds with extreme agony, and I can no longer live in absolute silence. Rising nausea threatens at the sight of anything edible, and I have become as thin as a rake, with my bones pressing out from beneath my skin. The anxiety is as bad as ever. It corners my consciousness with uncontrollable fear, creating hallucinations that have me cowering. I see death in every frame. Its insidious grip has haunted me for the last few days. The onslaught of its brutal symptoms weather me away. I am travelling back to where I came from, less determined than ever. I smell her perfume on my skin again. I see the marks she left on my arm, like ink on paper. I always scratch at the sight of it. I see her face when I close my eyes. I see the outline of her iris's form in all sorts of beautiful shapes. I hear her soft voice repeating itself inside of my skull, over and over and fucking over again. *But it isn't Leah anymore.* It's become Yasmin. She has consumed me. Eaten my heart. And her sudden disappearance took away an irreplaceable part of me. It is almost as if she took Leah with her, and left me with nothing but memories of the last months. And I look at God. He shows me what I could have never become. Sudden visions of life get fed into my head. Moments where I was nothing but a hollow shell. Moments of relief mixed with stress. And I peer into the present. But it's blank. There isn't anything there. I trail behind empty promises. I've dug a deep grave for myself.

The day went on like normal. It was cloudy. I went to pick up some medication. We took the car. It took us around thirty-five minutes to get there and come back. Leah wasn't acting normal, and it had been noticeable for days. But I let her be. It was always been better to just let her be. She had been distant for a while. I thought it would pass. It didn't but I tried not to think too much about it. I had been wanting to say something for the past few days. I never did. I inflicted so much harm on her I felt like I wasn't allowed to complain. It wouldn't have been fair. It was a few months after our break. I got fired from that dogpiss job, so she decided to forget about what happened and came back to live with me. I wasn't a good person that day. But I don't think I owe anybody a good person.

"There's something that I need to tell you, Noah," she said.

"Is it bad?"

"Yes," she said.

"Is it about us?"

"Yes," she answered.

And we began to drive back. I had a sinking feeling within me. We drove for around ten minutes in pure silence, and when I went to put my hand on her leg, she told me not to.

"Don't touch me."

"Why Leah? What's going on with you?"

"You won't want to after I tell you what happened."

And that's when shit dropped. And I remember that drive back home feeling like an eternity. It took too long. And we got home. We went into the kitchen. I was standing by the kitchen table, hands resting on it. And I asked what happened.

"I'm pregnant, Noah."

I looked at her. I wanted to kiss her badly. And she started crying, hard. I would finally become a father. I could correct my mistakes. I was now bound to her. A gift from God. A curse for blessings. I could be better than Papa. I could break the chain. But that wasn't it. She stood looking at me with unease, rubbing her arm up and down.

"It's not yours."

"What?"

"Noah, please."

"It's not mine?!" I angrily said.

"I've been with someone else."

"What do you mean? You fucked someone else?"

"For fucks sake! Yes. It's not yours Noah!"

And I remember being so fucking angry. And at that exact moment, I felt like I could kill her. I lost it. I lost it all at that exact moment. I lost purpose. With everything that I had done for her, she decided to brutally fuck me up. Everything that makes a meaningful life was so far out of reach that I felt like I could sacrifice it all. All I wanted was a kid. She knew this. But she always told me she never wanted one. How could she do this to me? How the fuck could she do this to me?

"Who is it?"

"I'm breaking up with you. I'll pack my stuff—" she calmly said.

"WHO THE FUCK IS IT?"

"Noah. We're done."

"Tell me who the fuck it is."

"I don't love you anymore Noah. Please, let me go," she pleaded.

"After everything we've been through, this is how you repay me?"

"Do you seriously think you're so innocent in all of this?"

I started slamming the countertop, slightly cracking it. I could see the fear in her eyes. Again.

"Forget about your stuff. Get out."

And she did. Breathe in and out. I won't be okay. That's for sure.

I see pain grate the skin off my body to unravel my true self, in pure peeled flesh. My vision has become narrower with each passing second. So has my will to live. White bandages are used to cover grave mistakes. Now deep red stains are left washed through them. There is mastery in the burdens I place upon myself. Restless nights are consumed with the suffering of rejecting the alcohol, but it will provide conformity to the social normalities that surround me. Things have only got worse, but I am learning to accept my distasteful subsistence. Fucking pathetic. Between everything there is less than nothing. I speak with no conviction. The distress of my being slowly fading into life's cruel existence contradicts what seems to be an everlasting journey. There isn't anything else to continue for. Only the slow hum of busy conversation with groans of loss keeps my ears perked high, and keeps me, to a certain extent, stable. I have become more fragile. Through it all I am shattering, because between everything there is still less than nothing. I have shredded any last hope of a return to who I was long ago. I have become someone unrecognisable even to my inner thoughts. All that is left is less than nothing. And it will stay that way.

I peer at the brown-bricked buildings, with dark streets illuminating more than the light would. The place I have found myself in is at the exact midpoint of here and home. According to the GPS. I can hear the wind caressing metal. And the slight drizzle is only visible through the scorching headlights. The smoke of my cigarette clouds the brink of whatever the fuck I am standing on. There is nothing to be seen ahead of me. Neither behind me. I appear to be anchored in a valley of subconscious torment. And in my restless nights, I see the same valley. Clearer. Clearer. It appears almost vividly real. Am I losing a fracture of my mind? Is my brain bleeding? Conflict keeps raging on inside of me. It fuels its inner war. It decapitates me. And it hurts whenever and wherever you touch it. But you have to touch it. It is obvious. People have bled for it. The way the wolf licks gently and passionately at the open wounds of its prey. I should have warned everyone away from myself.

Do you remember our woven cloth.

I feel a vibration in my pocket. I hastily grab my phone. I flip it open. An SMS lights up the bright screen.

"This is an automatic message from Life & Recovery Hill clinic. We're reaching out regarding your recent booking with us, made by Yasmin Atali. Please reply to confirm, and we will be sure to provide you with further details."

Fuck. A rush of blood rises to my head. I flinch at the sight of her name. I can't believe it. But in truth, I like to feel her again. True peace. Was this a sign from God? I am here. I lean against the hood of my car. I have accepted too little for too long. But this message came too late. I have made terrible mistakes. More terrible than any man should be capable of. But I have made them. I have let go of beautiful things for it. Just to be alive. But what do I know? The clinic shouldn't be too far away from here. I've heard about it before. And she knew where I came from. I check the address on my phone. A forty-minute walk from my current location. I start heading towards it and I almost believe I can start again. For a mere moment. The streets are silent. My footsteps make sound against the stoned pavement. Closed shutters at every window. Bad faith. There is a presence in the air. It makes breathing more difficult by the second. I feel like I'm being stared at, from all directions, through the shutters, through the glass and vines, through the trees and foliage. Their heads turn on the man walking isolated. But my head is placed between her collar and jaw. And there's no weight at all.

Take me back. Don't turn your back on me again. I'll show you that you'll need me.

I hope you'll need me eventually.

Life & Recovery Hill Clinic. A discreet sign displays the clinic's name. I let out a puff of smoke. It looks clean. Well-kept. It reassures me, somehow. Soothing shades of blue and grey outline the white walls. Green plants and colourful flowers flank the entrance. I can hear their cries. The mimicking of the sounds of people that have been welcomed in here. Sometimes I can feel my bones crack under the weight of them solely because I am one of them. I realise I am caught in the middle. I have no interest in going in. Why would I? I am doing fine on my own. But sometimes that isn't enough. Most of the time it isn't. My hands are fucking trembling. It takes a crisis to get to know another crisis. My absence doesn't bother me anymore. The blood doesn't taste the same. It's poison. I need the sickness inside of me. It stops me from deforming. Into change. It's eating up my nerves. I can never be normal. There isn't a place on this fucking earth where I can be seen as normal. And I'm abandoning everything around me. And that way I will never again be able to be abandoned. I truly believe that. I believe that. I should have been more like Papa. Gripping bathroom sinks. Popping more corks out of more bottles. Substantial violence. Staring into oblivion. Cold hugs. Distance. So much distance. Finding disapproval where I showed weakness. When I wasn't enough of a man. When he would hit me. Repeatedly. Until my arm would turn purple through the bruises he laid on me. It worked. It really worked. And I would cry. And he would force me not to. I was still young. I didn't understand why he would do these things. Now I do. Maybe it's my father's sadness. Maybe his grief. Maybe both. That was his mercy towards me. It was unbearable. I'm glad I wasn't made a father. What would I even be? Will I teach them what Papa's father taught him? After all, I am his son. Will they find themselves in the sweat and tears and blood and alcohol of my grief. Will they rejoice in it. Will they fucking rejoice in it. I would never be able to fit those shoes. I am somehow the sin of my father. Hopefully, my gravestone will show more signs of warmth. But it doesn't matter. I can't enter this place. I drive off. And I find it difficult to figure out what I need. As long as I stay away from everything that isn't myself. I black out.

God willing.

———

Slow-burning. My eyes slowly open to the sound of a low hum. Blood pressure cuffs tight around my arms and the sharp point of the needle digs inside of my vein. There are sharp scratches in my head, and they're pounding their way out. It's itching. It takes me a second to remember what happened. Somebody must have found me passed out. They should have left me out there. I don't want to be here. Sometimes I don't want to heal any more than I've done already. Why can't people fucking understand that? It's the last thing I have left. It's all I am. I've seen my sun darkened. The pain hooked into my skin. Insensibility. I'd rather make an enemy of everyone than doubt who I am. I don't know who I am without it. It's built a home within me. I look around the room. There isn't much. The paint is coming off of the walls. There is a sink. It's rusted. The bed I'm lying on is just big enough for me. My feet touch the edge. And there's a white wardrobe against the wall. The door opens, slowly, and a man dressed in all-white steps in.

"Good evening Noah Algazi. How are you feeling?"

I groan as I try to sit up. The room is spinning

"I'm okay. Can I leave?"

"That's why I'm here. I'm discharging you."

Silence follows, amplified by the slow ticking of the clock on the wall. A single window lets in a dull grey light. My throat becomes dry. My voice cracks as I try to speak.

"But where will I go? I don't have anywhere to stay."

"I'm sorry, but that's not up to us. We can't decide that for you."

The man struggles to make eye contact with me. He moves around like a crackhead.

"We need the bed, Noah."

"Isn't there any possibility you can just move me to another room?"

Why the fuck would I want to leave. I'm in control here. I can be helped.

"I know it's hard but we have no reason to keep you any longer. There are other patients with more life-threatening issues. We have social workers that can try and help you find some—"

"I'm not okay in the head, man. I need this. I'm fucking human too," I reply, stuttering my way through.

His face says it all. There's the shame. The judgement. Even if he doesn't mean to show it. I can see it. He doesn't see me as a person. I need him to extend a hand. But he doesn't. He just sighs.

"I know. But it's all we can do."

He stands next to the bed and places his hand on my shoulder. I flinch.

"Get off me," I say.

"Please, Noah. Relax for a bit," he says.

"Relax? How the fuck can I relax. Do you know how many times I've tried to be helped? Do you have any idea? I'm tired, man. Of feeling detached. I just want some help."

He backs off. I rip the needle out of my arm. Small trickles of blood fall on the white covers of the bed. I take the rest of the machinery off and I stand up. I support myself against the wall and make my way to the wardrobe. I take out my clothes and signal to be left alone. He leaves. And I get changed. I see myself in the mirror. And there is no virginal innocence left. I have been used up. Beaten. Broken. Bandaged. Fixed. Beaten. Broken. Bandaged. Fixed. I fear my reflection. And as it peers back at me I can't even recognise it. I hold my face in my hands. I don't see anything of my own. My uneven shoulders show the imbalance of recovery. I feel my jaw clench tight. I hit the mirror, and the shards of glass penetrate my hand. I don't think there has been a single moment of understanding since I was seven. I am composed of illness. I am the residue of a stranger's cigarette. Glass lies all around the floor, and I try to step back without it hurting my feet any more than it already has. I don't waste time. I head out of the room, into a thin stretched corridor. I don't know which way I'm going, but I take a left turn. I get to the waiting room. It's crowded. But I can breathe without her lingering on my lips here. Nothing can be littered here. I hope to never return.

I'm still looking for closure. Have you noticed?

I derail myself. Over and over. People pass by in blurred lines of colour and shape. And at every angle, there is more to it. Hundreds of lines. Strangers. Yet every single one has an entire life. Hidden. Secrets. Corruption. Desire. Money. None. Faith. Family. Dreams. Problems. Issues. They've loved, cried, hurt and gone through it all. Yet the world and I always miss out on each other. We don't acknowledge our existence the way we are supposed to. Maybe they all hate each other as much as I hate myself. Or maybe they don't feel like I do. Maybe not. Each person that walks by, is a second too late or early to be remembered. Forgotten. For a brief moment. Different destinations that end or begin with different journeys. Connections. Train lines. I derail myself. Complexity. Swallowing. Pure disappointment. And I still had the balls to try. I showed up there, didn't I? I showed up. I mattered. I mattered for whatever it was worth. But I've always decided to go against the grain. I find myself going in a direction honest and true. What if everyone else is wrong? Is this my way out? It looks like I'm about to burst into tears. Suicidal. Shiftless. Softbrained. Yet I peer through the foliage. Ever so carefully. And I know there is nothing left for me. I have to head back home. To where I belong. Outside of the city. Away from the people and the sound and the connections and lines and corrections. The extremes of despair. But there isn't anything left to do. I should head back home and let that place take care of me. That should be good for me. I'm not sure anything else will help. I have to head back home. Something is awaiting me. I know something is.

Even if I could find her again. It would take seconds for me to run it straight into the muddied ground.

Chapter 7
Summer Of 2007

The sight of the old-found neighbourhood brings a slight crease of a smile to my face. The overarching trees still sway gently in the morning wind, and the apartment block still stands as if nothing has ever changed. God's palace is still radiating its faith. Its towers still stand arisen. As the road bends and weaves around the mountain, I recognise familiar ground. I have never really left. I was only temporarily gone. Home is found where you never are. At least that's my experience of it. Sometimes you have to leave. To fall apart from what you know to realise how badly you need to get back. No one leaves home. Until it pleads in your ear. It begs you to leave. To save yourself. To run away from home. Anywhere was safer than here. It pulls you at your limbs. It rips you apart, slowly, and makes you scream to be let go. I have folded grief. I have put it between the slabs of stones. In the walls. Between the rubble. This is where I have been known to be. Where I have birthed revelation and been bereaved. The place where different versions are hung as corpses among the trees. And where the sun filters through the empty eye sockets onto me. These walls have heard prayers. I could never be a stranger here. It has seen my soul. It has ripped it out of me. And even after change, it's created the absence of me.

Isn't it beautiful that our eyes blur the truth?

———

I stand. Outside. Stuck in place. I am losing it. Seeing everything. I am seeing everything. I get the same feeling you get when you visit a familiar place. But after dusk. Familiarity, but disguised. I don't get to know. I only know that when I leave this world everything around me will outlast me. And I am grateful. The blank sky is covered with clouds. I dig my fingernails into my arm. I scratch. I tear. I am idle. I manage to enter the building. The entrance is still the same. Everything is still the same. I make my way upstairs. The key turns in the lock. The apartment has been raided. The mattress is flipped. And everything I left behind has been thrown around carelessly. I walk around in circles. I am relieved. But I am still troubled.

Leah. Leah. Leah.

Sweat starts to form on my palms and hands, and I drop to my knees. Her face brings back the flood. The arch of our existence extends outwards. She was never the problem holding me back. I thought hell on earth was found in the tragic shape of her. We had a love so fundamentally deep that it had to be eradicated. I never wanted to get better. I despised the idea of being the person I was before she showed up. Everything is clear. I remember letting her eyes rest in mine. I felt the sense of her betrayal rush through me. Her sharp scream cut the tension in the air. I lifted my arm, shaking, and the bullet dug itself deep into her skull. And that was it. I saw both our lives flash by. I couldn't take it. I couldn't let her live without me. I couldn't let myself sacrifice my worth for hers. I held her. And that was it. Blood dripped onto the pavement. It formed a puddle at my feet. I tried to stop the bleeding. I couldn't. It kept coming out of the small puncture. How can a man deal with the fact that there's an end to everything. She stopped existing. And that was it.

"What the fuck," I mumble, realising I've been holding my breath. I let out a trembling sigh, and with it, my heart skips its usual rhythmic beat. My hands were covered with the crimson essence of her being. I cried at her side. For a mere hour. I did think about it. But I think I still knew all along she wouldn't fulfil me. And she never did. She never truly loved me. She loved the idea of me being around, for her to feel better about herself. To see me wither away into ash and dust. That is what she loved. To feel superior. To be better. Was that it? Was that really it? Or was she consumed by the fear that I would always stay the same. Consumed by the idea of travelling the same path over and fucking over again so many times that we became well-worn, and used up by each other. The rain drained the blood into the gutter. I remember placing the gun in her hand. I was stressed out of my damn mind. I dialled the emergency services. I pretended I found her, like I didn't see it happen. I drew a portrait of suicide. There was no mental preparation. It happened so quickly. Even until the last moment, I knew I was soliciting death. Was it the alcohol's fault? It couldn't have been mine. I don't know what took over me. My mind had erased the whole situation. There has always been a vague desire to take back my life. I treated that sentence too well. I thought I found her that way. I never did. I was fucking there. And since then I never came back to my senses. I remember. I've always remembered. Clarity was hidden away from me. It couldn't have been my fault. Clear accountability hidden behind addiction. The grief I feel has become so infinitely soft. It rests upon my temple. It has become its own permanent mark. A wedding with the life I must live. A settlement through death. A trembling voice with nothing to say other than sorrowful words. Once anything begins, there are only endings to be frightened of. I've been holding this secret in plain sight. Its power only lies within my truth. My corrupted truth. I have become my enemy. I cannot save myself. And her image, which was kept sacred, is starting to disintegrate into horror. Her shadow still blankets over me. I stay on my knees.

"I'm sorry. I'm so fucking sorry," I whisper.

A womb. Stranded. Once full of life, but now lifeless.

The wind rustled through the grassy field. The sun was slowly fading away, but there was enough light left to last a day. She was looking straight at it. But I was looking at her. She noticed me staring. And her sight always falls upon my scars.

"We can't simply lie here and keep staring at our wounds together"

"I know," she said quietly.

"I know you know."

"Why can't we do that though? We're all we have. And besides I haven't been able to get this day out of my head."

"Okay Leah," I said, unable to hold my smile back.

I put a cigarette behind my ear.

"I think God doesn't like talking to me," she whispered.

"Did you sit with Him?"

"I beg. I cry. I pray. But I never get served anything good."

I see tears form on her cheeks.

"Do you sometimes resent the things you see in me?" Leah says.

"Oh, what?"

"Do I make you remember?"

"What are you talking about—"

"Do I make you remember all of the bad I've said towards you?"

"Uh, I'm still here," I said as my voice slightly trembled at the weight of the words.

"That wasn't my—"

"That's my answer"

"Noah, there's always a reason for people to carry so much hate"

"I don't resent you, Leah. I don't have any reason to. Right?"

I looked at her. Her eyes burned through mine.

"Of course not," she laughingly said.

But her tone changed.

"We can't permit all this hatred to fuck us up like the way it does."

"Yeah, I guess."

"Let's not pay attention to the end of things. Morning always comes back around, right? And we got each other when the world ends. I think that matters."

"I want everything."

"Like what?" I answered.

"I want you to ruin me. I want you to go so far that I need you to live."

"Leah. I don't think I can ruin you."

"I want to be part of you."

She ran her hand along the underside of my arm. And as she did, she crept up against my side. I turned my head to face her. I could see insects crawl in between us. There was a lot of life present. She would have swallowed the sun for me if she could.

"I can't stop thinking about you. It's constant. I don't know if I deserve you," I said.

"Why Noah?"

"It scares me that you're nothing but love."

I forgave the world because it had her in it. But then it passed. What were we?

I knock on Elias's door. I wonder what his reaction will be to seeing me. Hopefully, I don't startle him too much.

"Hello, how can I help you?" a faint male voice says. But the man doesn't open the door. He carefully keeps his distance. I don't blame him. He doesn't know me, and I don't know him. New residents?

"Is Elias home? I'm an old... friend of his."

"Oh, my gosh."

A long silence follows. A man opens up the door. He looks to be in his early sixties. Grey strands sit in between darker tones of hair. He looks at me with teary eyes.

"Come in."

"Oh, I don't mean to intrude or anything."

"You must be Noah."

"Yeah," I say, confused.

Elias's father. I never met him before. He wasn't around much. At least not to my direct knowledge. Elias didn't talk about him.

"Please, sit."

The apartment doesn't look any different than the last time I was here. It almost seems like both of us are intruding.

"How are you, Noah?"

"I'm doing fine. Where is Elias?"

His heavy demeanour seems to carry a lot of weight. He looks down and doesn't immediately answer.

"He passed, Noah."

I don't know what to say. My heart drops. My rib cage stings at the thought of it.

"My son tried hard, Noah. Really hard. He got better. He stopped using. He waited— he waited a long time to get better. And then—"

He puts his palms on his face. He starts to sob but continues to talk through it.

"And then he decided to join the army. I hated him for it. I couldn't forgive him for it. Not for a while. He tried to contact me multiple times. I ignored his calls, Noah. I never once picked up. He didn't even make it out of boot camp. His best friend got shot. It was a horrible accident. And Elias witnessed it all. He couldn't deal with what he saw. He took his own life."

"I am so sorry..." I manage to say.

"And his two kids. They're still babies."

"He has kids?"

I can see the pained look on his face. It's almost like I'm looking through to Elias's last moments. I see his face, laced with fear. I imagine his wife facing the news of his passing. And I think about his lifeless body, probably thousands of kilometres away, staining foreign sand red. And how he was probably judged for it. I wish I could've done more. But he's gone. My mistakes are forever ingrained within him. But that was a long time ago. It shouldn't matter any more. Things cannot only matter when they are too late to be changed. And I still can't let it go. I still can't let it go. It's not my place any more.

"He left something for you. Something he wanted you to read."

He stands up and walks to a brown cupboard. He opens up the top drawer and reaches inside. He hands me a half-opened envelope. It has a paper inside. It reads;

"After that talk we had it changed something within me cause I've gone through it all right under everybody's nose and nobody has ever had the decency to just listen and put me on the right track. So thank you. Even though I don't forgive you for the things you said to me, forgive yourself, Noah. You've had it bad, and that's enough of an excuse. I think we both deserve a good epilogue. We've both suffered enough, haven't we?"

There's a lot of sadness within me. He was a good person. He always was. We always have the power to offer someone else some sort of relief. I've withheld from doing that. For my own sake. And I don't know if I will be able to forgive myself. It feels like a lot. Just to get some relief is all he asked. I don't know why he thanked me. I guess he had too much love in his heart.

"Can you spare me a hug, man?"

Without question, I stand up and embrace him. He holds me tight. I hold him back, tightly too. Is this what it feels like? To find fragments of what you never had in other people. In strangers, you don't even know. But we are connected through suffering. I pull away. I clutch my chest. I whimper like a wounded dog. His father seems like a good man. It makes my stomach turn. Sometimes I wish things could stay how they always were. Sometimes things shouldn't change, just so I can prove to myself that it was all real. What I am is real. And what Elias was is still real. It lives within my caves. It comes and goes. It always comes and goes. There is no greater desire than living a life where things stay. He hugs me again.

I wish I had a father like his.

I head back to my apartment. I left the door open on a crack and the key is still in the lock. I enter. Overwhelmed, I let myself fall back on the mattress. Stains cover the creamy white of it. My fingers trace the crooked lines of the mattress, and I let them run along the edge of it. I sigh, with effort. I pull out my necklace, and I clutch the golden Star of David hanging at the end of it. I pray for Mama. There isn't much left I can do any more. I've had a life. I've spent it like an irresistible urge. I've let it waste me away. But that is just how it goes. And I've let it do that. I look up to the ceiling as the afternoon comes in. The sun hangs high. Incomprehensible states. There isn't one nerve in my body that can handle what I've done. I grip harder on my necklace. I can't blame anyone else. There is nowhere left to turn. I'll never be what I was supposed to be. I think I understand now. The consequence will be pleasurable. Small droplets of blood fall from my hand. The edges of the Star of David have pierced my skin. In no way am I perfect, and I never really wanted to be. The bleak colours of the room no longer find solace in the brown walls. Cigarette buds still stain the carpet with heavy black strokes. I remember this place. It used to be my safe haven, a delicate abode where I could unravel myself and lay it down with ease. But it no longer is. Regret still takes me above the threshold, and I find disappointment with what I am. The remains of Leah have faded into dust. I hold myself accountable for the pain I have caused. I will never forgive. I feel proud that I won't. It has given me some good purpose. Some goodwill. To be in love with someone no longer there, when curtains are drawn and everything is in darkness, and to hold it with a grudge-bearing caress to show what I could have never become. I feel God's gaze. It is shameful for me to be alive. Through the bitterness, I know what I have to do.

I sit with my back against the wall. I pick up the firearm I have kept heavily close. I open my mouth wide. *Mama?* I press the barrel against the roof. *I rasp. My throat hurts.* Saliva drips on chrome. *I don't think it's safe for me to be who I am.* My finger rests on the trigger. *You should confront your buried self.* I push with a faint bit of pressure. I don't let it take me. I don't go through with it. I stand up, and I stumble over to the kitchen. I look under the sink and there is still a bottle of alcohol. I drink the whole thing down. I then head to the bedroom, and I unzip the bag. I find the painkillers for my headache. This is a better way out. I sit on the mattress. I empty out all the pills onto the palm of my hand. Everything is silent. The noise stops. I look into the nothingness and I swallow them down. I lie down. I keep my eyes open. And they stay open as they suffer a final blink.

It is the summer of 2007. Nobody cared to ask me if I was ready for all of this.

We only briefly occupy our chairs. Everything someday ends, and now is when everything does. Grief rests its head in a small town, upon a hill, in a crestfallen apartment I will now forever call my home.